IN THE
BOSS'S CASTLE

IN THE
BOSS'S CASTLE

BY

JESSICA GILMORE

MILLS
BOON

First published in Great Britain 2016
By Mills & Boon, an imprint of HarperCollins*Publishers*
1 London Bridge Street, London, SE1 9GF

Large Print edition 2016

© 2016 Jessica Gilmore

ISBN: 978-0-263-26236-0

Printed and bound in Great Britain
by CPI Antony Rowe, Chippenham, Wiltshire

For Audrey, Rob, Josh, Michaela and Lily.
With much love always. x

PROLOGUE

Hi, Hope,
Truthfully I was a little shocked when they asked me to job swap with you for six months. I thought I was way too far down the food chain, especially since I changed careers and found myself back at the bottom of the ladder again. But I've never left the US—so my bags are packed, I actually have a pass-port and I'm on my way to London before they change their minds!

I guess you want to know a little about the stranger coming to take over your life? There's no big scandals you'll be glad to know, so no need to warn the neighbours or hide the family silver. I'm Maddison and I've been working for DL Media for just over three years, I started out in the PR and events team before Brenda, my boss (soon to be yours) poached me for Editorial. It's a step down in some ways—back to making coffees and booking taxis and a lot less managing my own time, but somehow she convinced me that it'll be worth it. It's nice to be wanted for my brains and not my contact list, at least that's what I tell myself when I pick up her dry cleaning. Because, in between the taxis and the coffee pick-ups, she is teaching me a lot—you're lucky to be working with her.

She's very focused, doesn't see the point of any life outside work and is absolutely obsessed with glass ceilings and reaching full potential, blah-blah-blah. It's not that I don't want all that, I'm as ambitious as they come in some ways, but I do want more. I want it all. I want to meet the right guy and settle down, picket fence, big dog, rugrats and all. Don't tell Brenda that!

I thought I'd found the right guy. Bart. AKA Bartholomew J Van De Grierson III. But turns out he's not The One or rather I'm not The One for him. At least not right now. He wants a break. Thinks we should 'explore other options'. So this opportunity has come at the right time for me. I'm exploring other options on the other side of the Atlantic and putting my career first for a change. Maybe working with Brenda has influenced me more than I knew!

I do hope he misses me at least a little, though...

So—New York! It's the greatest city on earth, I promise. My biggest advice? Pack light! The good news is you'll be living in the Upper East Side and it is fabulous! The bad news? No one expects to swing a cat in a New York studio, but mine...? You couldn't swing a mouse. But, hey, location is everything, right? And when you sit on the fire escape with your morning coffee and watch the sun rise over Manhattan you won't want to be anywhere else.

Welcome to New York. City of reinvention, city of dreams...
Maddison.

Hi, Maddison...
Welcome to London and London's greatest borough. I've compiled a 'Welcome' file

which tells you absolutely everything you need to know, in alphabetical order, from where the boiler is—and the number of a good plumber—to the best place to buy coffee locally. There's a guide to buses and Oyster cards (no Tube here in Stokey) under T for Transport, and a comprehensive section on work (W for Work) to help you find your feet right away.

I hope you feel at home here. Stoke Newington is pretty sought-after now, but when my parents moved here it was still a scruffy, community-minded part of the East End—and even with all the swanky bars and yoga studios I miss the place I grew up in. Not so community-minded when you are more likely to bump into nannies and cleaners than neighbours, and everyone is obsessed with extending and rainforest wetrooms. But it's still home and I can't imagine living anywhere else. Except maybe New York, of course...

I am so excited about moving to New York for a whole six months. I've always wanted to travel but never had the opportunity. Faith, my younger sister, is on a gap year and seeing the world, lucky thing—but living in a new city and progressing my career? That's an amazing opportunity.

I've also been at DL Media for around three years. Before that I was working at a local solicitors' firm which fitted in with Faith's school hours. But as soon as she was old enough for me to commute to work I came to DL, at first as a general PA, before getting the opportunity to work with Kit Buchanan as an editorial assistant.

Brenda sounds like just what I need—a real mentor. Kit, your boss-to-be, is... Well, he's brilliant. Everyone agrees with that. It's just I'm not sure he ever sees me. Sometimes I feel like I'm just a piece of efficient office furniture.

In fact it's been a really long time since anyone has seen me as anyone worth knowing. It gets a little lonely, to be honest, especially now that Faith is making it very clear that now she's grown up she doesn't need me to fuss over her.

Maybe she's right. Maybe it's time to put me first.

Starting with New York!

Enjoy London.

Love, Hope x

CHAPTER ONE

MADDISON CARTER OPENED the opaque glass door, leaned against the door frame and held up her perfectly manicured hand, a piece of paper dangling from her fingertips. 'Messages,' she announced.

Kit Buchanan pushed his chair away from his desk and blinked at her. His expression might seem sleepy and unconcerned to the casual observer but after just four weeks Maddison knew better. 'You could email them to me,' he suggested, a teasing gleam in his blue eyes. This conversation was getting as predictable as the sunrise. So she used paper and a pen and preferred her lists on thick white paper, not on an electronic device? It didn't make her a Luddite, it made her efficient.

'And have you ignore them? I think not.'

Kit sighed. The soft *here she goes again* sigh he used about this time every day. 'But, Maddison, maybe I like ignoring messages.' His eyes laughed up at her but she refused to smile back, even a little. She wasn't colluding with him.

'Then get an answering service. Or a machine or just answer your cell phone every once in a while and then I...' she brandished the list '...I wouldn't have to tell your girlfriends that you're in a meeting twenty times a day.'

His eyebrows rose. 'Twenty times? How very keen.'

Okay, she might have exaggerated slightly but just one conversation with the terribly polite and terribly condescending Camilla was enough and three definitely enough to drive the most precise person to hyperbole. Maddison ignored the interruption and, in a deliberately slow voice, began to read from the paper. 'Right, your mother called and said please call her back, today, and confirm you are going to the wedding, it's a three-line whip and if you don't RSVP soon she will do it for you. Your sister called and said, and I quote, "Tell him if I have to go to this damn wedding on my own I will make him suffer in ways he can't even imagine and don't think I won't do it..."'

Maddison paused as she reread the words. She liked the sound of Kit's sister, Bridget, with her soft, lilting voice and steely words.

'And Camilla called three times, can you please answer your cell, how can she expect to get ready for a wedding in just a couple of weeks if you won't even confirm that you're taking her, you inconsiderate bas…' She looked up and allowed herself one brief smile. 'I didn't catch the rest of that sentence.'

'The hell you didn't,' he said softly. The smile still curved his mouth and he was still leaning back in the vast, black leather chair but the glint had disappeared from his eyes. 'Everyone seems *very* keen to make sure I attend this wedding.'

'If you would just RSVP they'd stop calling.' Maddison didn't care whether he went to the darn wedding or not. She just wanted to stop fielding calls about it.

'I will, as soon as I've decided.'

'Decided?'

'Whether I'm going or not.'

Maddison heaved a theatrical sigh. 'Great. Can I beg you to do just one thing? Put Camilla out of her misery.' Sure, the woman spoke to Maddison as if she were some sort of servant, and sure, she sounded like a snooty character in a Hugh Grant movie, all clipped vowels and lots of long *r*'s, but she was getting a little more desperate with every call. Maddison would never allow herself to beg for a man's attention but she knew all too well what it felt like to see the spark die even as she did her best to keep it going. Knew what it felt like to see the emails and texts diminish, hear the call go straight to voicemail.

Kit stared at her, his eyes narrowed. 'I didn't know that advising on my personal life was in your job description.'

Maddison took a deep breath, willing herself to stay calm. 'Nor did I and yet here I am, taking calls from your girlfriend eight hours a day.'

'Ex-girlfriend.'

'She...what?'

His eyes caught hers, the blue turned steely. 'Ex-girlfriend. She just wants to come to the wedding. Thinks if I take her to meet the parents then things might start again between us. So you see, I'm not a total git.'

Whatever *that* might be. Maddison stared down at the list, her righteous indignation draining away. 'Okay. I apologize—although in my defence it seems that Camilla doesn't understand the *ex* part of your relationship. Maybe she needs reminding. And you *really* should call your mother.'

He didn't respond for a long moment and Maddison kept her eyes on the list, knowing she had gone too far. She was normally so good at keeping her cool but Kit Buchanan was just so...so *provoking*.

She started at his unexpected laugh. 'There are times when you remind me of my school matron. I will, I promise. How are things looking for tonight?'

The abrupt turn of subject was a relief. She had spent far too long today on Kit Buchanan's social life; work was a much safer subject. Maddison looked at her list again, composing herself as she did so. 'The caterers are already there and setting up, so are the bar staff. The warehouse confirmed that they have sent two hundred books across ready for the signing. I got late acceptances from five people, their names have been added to the entrance list and the door staff are primed; three people sent in late apologies, I re-

plied on your behalf and arranged for books and
goody bags to be sent to their offices. Oh, and I
popped into the venue last night after work and
took a last look around. Everything is in order.'

'Very efficient, as always, thank you, Maddison.' The words were perfect but the amusement in his tone took the edge off his praise and
despite herself she could feel her cheeks flush.
Kit always seemed to be laughing at her and it
was…unsettling. She wanted respect, not this
knowing humour. But so far, no matter what she
did, respect seemed to be eluding her. And, dam-
mit, it rankled. She was usually so much better
at impressing the right people in the right ways.

She certainly wasn't used to feeling discom-
bobulated several times a day.

She eyed her boss. He was still lounging back
in his chair, an unrepentant gleam in his eye
as he waited for her response. Hoping that she
would lose her cool, no doubt. Well, she wasn't
going to give him the satisfaction but, oh, her
fingers curled; it was tempting.

It didn't help that Kit was young—ish. Handsome if you liked brown tousled hair that needed
a good cut, dark stubble and blue eyes, if you

found scruffy chic, like some hipster cross between a college professor and an outdoorsman, attractive. Maddison didn't. She liked her men clean-cut, clean-shaven and well turned out.

But, even if he wore head-to-toe *couture*, Kit Buchanan still wouldn't be her type. *Bart* was her type: tall, athletic, with a good job in banking, a trust fund and a bloodline that ran back to Edith Wharton's innocent age and beyond. Not to mention the brownstone. Breaking up with the brownstone was almost harder than saying goodbye to the man. She'd invested eighteen months in that relationship, spent eighteen months moulding herself into the perfect consort. All for nothing. She was back at square one.

Although, he *had* said a break. Maddison clung on to those words, hope soothing the worry and doubt clawing her insides. Everyone knew that taking a break wasn't the same thing as breaking up. And if Bart saw that she was having an amazing time in London without him then surely he would realize he had made a very big mistake? Maybe this distance, this time apart was a good thing, the push he needed to take things to the next level.

She just needed to start *having* the amazing time. So far Maddison's London experiences had been confined to work, takeaways and working her way through Hope McKenzie's formidable box-set collection. Watching *Sex and the City* instead of living it. Surely she at least deserved to be *flirting* in the city?

Kit's voice brought her back to her present surroundings—thousands of miles away from her unexpected failure. 'Anything else on that list of yours or is it all neatly ticked and crossed out?'

Okay. This was it. She'd spent the last four weeks regrouping, licking her wounds, grateful for the opportunity to recover and plan far away from the all-too-knowing eyes of her New York social group. She'd been so *sure* of Bart, shown her hand too early and lost spectacularly. But it was time to reassert herself, professionally at least. Then maybe she would get her confidence—and her man—back. Maddison willed herself to sound composed, her voice not to tremble. 'I think you should rewrite your speech for tonight.'

Kit went very still, like a predator watching his prey. 'Oh? Why?'

'It's very clinical.' She kept her eyes focused on him even as her knees trembled and every instinct screamed at her to stop talking and to back out of the door before she got her ass fired. 'You've spent the whole four weeks I've been here absolutely absorbed in your work. You barely noticed that Hope had gone. You've been in before me every morning, not stopped for lunch unless you had a meeting and who knows what time you leave? But the speech? It has no passion in it at all.'

Kit didn't take his eyes off her, his face utterly expressionless. 'Have you read it? The book?'

Had she what? 'I...of course.'

'Could you do a better job?'

She flinched at the cold words, then tossed her head up and glared at him. 'Could I write an introductory speech that sounds like I value the author, think the book is worth reading and convince the room that they need to read it too? Yes. Yes, I could.'

'Great.' He pulled his chair back to his desk

and refocused his eyes on his screen. 'You have an hour. Let's see what you come up with.'

'Great speech.'

Kit suppressed a sigh as yet another guest complimented him. It *had* been a great speech and he'd delivered it well, a nice mingling of humour and sincerity. Only he hadn't written it. Embellished it, ad-libbed a little but he hadn't written it. Maddison had been annoyingly right: his own effort had lacked passion.

Kit knew all too well why that was. Three years ago he'd lost any passion, any zest for life, any hope—and now it seemed as though he'd lost the ability to fake it as well.

Which was ridiculous. He was the king of faking it—at work, with the ever so elegant Camilla and her potential replacements, with his friends. The only place he couldn't convincingly pretend that he was the same old Kit was with his family. Especially not with his family and with the wedding looming on the horizon like a constant reminder of all that he had lost. He needed to sort that out and fast. He knew he had to RSVP. He knew he had to attend. He just couldn't bring himself to commit to it because once he did it would become real. Thank goodness for his new project. At least that helped him forget, for a little while at least.

Forgetting was a luxury.

He caught sight of Maddison, gliding through the crowds as untouchably serene as ever. Kit's eyes narrowed as she stopped to murmur something in a waitress's ear, sending the girl scurrying off with her tray. As usual Maddison had it all under control. Just look at the way she glided around the office in her monochrome uniform of black trousers and perfectly ironed white blouse like some sort of robot: efficient, calm and, until today, he could have sworn completely free of any emotion.

It was a shame. No one whose green eyes tilted upwards with such feline wickedness, no one with hair like the first hint of a shepherd's sunset, no one with a wide, sweet mouth should be so *bland*.

But she hadn't been so bland earlier today. Instead she had been bursting with opinions and, much as she had tried to stay calm, not let him see the exasperation in those thickly lashed eyes, she had let her mask slip a little.

And then she had written that speech. In an hour. Yes, she definitely had hidden depths. Not, Kit reminded himself, that he was planning to explore them. He was just intrigued, that was all. Turned out Maddison Carter was a bit of an enigma and he did so like to figure out a puzzle.

Kit excused himself from the group of guests, brushing another compliment about his speech aside with a smile and a handshake as he slowly weaved his way through the throng, checking to make sure everyone was entertained, that the buzz was sufficient to ensure the launch would be a success. The venue was inspired, an old art deco cinema perfectly complementing the novel's historical Jazz Age setting. The seats had been removed to create a party space and a jazz band set up on the old stage entertained the crowd with a series of jaunty tunes. Neon cocktails circulated on etched silver trays as light shone down from spotlights overhead, emphasizing the huge, jewel-coloured rectangular windows; at the far end of the room the gratified author sat at a vintage desk, signing books and holding court. The right people were here having the right sort of time. Kit had done all he could—the book would stand or fall on its own merits now.

He paused as Maddison passed by again, that damn list still tucked in one hand, a couple of empty glasses clasped in the other. He leaned against the wall for a moment, enjoying watching her dispose of the glasses, ensure three guests had fresh drinks, introduce two lost-looking souls to each other, all the while directing the wait staff and ensuring the queue for signed books progressed. A one-woman event machine.

How did she do it? She looked utterly calm, still in her favourite monochrome uniform although she had changed her usual well-tailored trousers for a short skirt, which swished most pleasingly around what were, Kit had to admit, a fine pair of legs, and there was no way the silky, clingy white blouse, which dipped to a low vee just this side of respectable, was the same as the crisp shirt she had worn in the office. Her hair was no longer looped in a loose knot but allowed to curl loosely around her shoulders. She looked softer, more approachable—even though she was brandishing the dreaded list.

She was doing a great job organizing this party. He really should go and tell her so while he remembered.

By the time Kit had manoeuvred his way over to Maddison's corner of the room she was deep in conversation with an earnest-looking man. Kit rocked back on his heels and studied her. Good gracious, was that a smile on her face? In fact, that dip of her head and the long demure look from under her eyebrows was positively flirtatious. Kit neatly collected two cocktails from a passing tray and watched as the earnest man slipped her a card. Did he know him? He knew almost every person there. Kit ran through his memory banks—yes, a reviewer for one of the broadsheets. Not a bad conquest, especially if she could talk him into positive reviews.

'Flirting on the job?' he said quietly into her ear as the earnest man walked away, and had the satisfaction of seeing her jump and the colour rush to her cheeks, emphasizing the curve in her heart-shaped face.

'No. I was just...'

'Relax, Maddison, I was teasing. It's past eight o'clock. I think you're on your own time now. This lot will melt away as soon as they realize that these are no longer being served.' He handed her the pink cocktail before tasting his own blue confection and grimaced as the sweet yet medicinal taste hit his tongue. 'Or maybe not. Is this supposed to taste like cough syrup? Anyway, cheers. Great job on the party.'

'Thank you.' It was as if a light had been switched on in her green eyes, turning them from pretty glass to a darker, more dangerous emerald. 'Hope started it all. I just followed her instructions.'

'The party favours were your idea, and the band, I believe.'

Her eyes lit up even more. 'I didn't know you'd noticed. It just seemed perfect, nineteen twenties and a murder mystery.' The guests' goody bags contained chocolate murder weapons straight out of a golden-age crime novel: hatpins and candlesticks, pearl-handled revolvers and a jar-shaped chocolate labelled Cyanide. The cute chocolates had caused quite a stir and several guests were trying to make sure they went home with a full

set. Turned out even this jaded crowd could be
excited by something novel and fun.

'Excuse me.'

Kit looked around, an enquiring eyebrow raised,
only for the young man hovering behind him to
ignore him entirely while he thrust a card in Maddison's direction. 'It was lovely to meet you earlier. Do give me a call. I would love to show you
around London. Oh, and happy birthday.'

'Thank you.' She accepted the card with a half-
smile, sliding it neatly into her bag. Kit tried to
sneak a look as the card disappeared into the
depths. How many other cards did she have in
there? And what had the young man said?

'It's your birthday?'

Maddison nodded. 'Today.'

'I didn't realize.' Kit felt strangely wrong-
footed. How hadn't he known? He'd always remembered Hope's birthday although, come to
think of it, that was because she made sure it
was in his work calendar and lost no opportunity to remind him that flowers were always acceptable, chocolates even more so and vouchers
for the local spa most acceptable of all. 'I'm so
sorry you had to work. I hope you have exciting
plans for the rest of your evening and weekend?'

Maddison paused, her eyes lowered. 'Sure.' But her tone lacked conviction.

'Like?' Kit cursed himself as he pushed. She'd said she had plans so he should take her word at face value and leave her in peace. He didn't need to know the details; she was a grown woman.

A grown woman in a new city where she knew hardly anyone.

Maddison took a visible deep breath before looking directly at him, a smile pasted on to her face. 'A film and a takeaway. I'm going to explore the city a little more tomorrow. Low-key, you know? I don't know many people here yet.'

'You're staying in alone, on your birthday?'

'I have a cocktail.' She waved the glass of pink liquid at him. 'It's okay.'

He'd heard the lady. She said she was okay—and, judging by the cards she was collecting, the room was full of men who would gladly help her celebrate any way she wished to.

Only she was new to the country... Kit had thought his conscience had died three years ago but some ghost of it was struggling back to life. 'What about the other girls at work? None of them free?'

'It's a little awkward, you know? Technically

I'm at the same level as all the other assistants but they all sit in the same office and I'm on the executive floor so we don't see each other day-to-day.' She hesitated. 'I think Hope didn't really socialize so there's this assumption I'm the same.' She shrugged. 'It's fine. I just haven't prioritized making friends since I got here. There's plenty of time.' She attempted another full smile; this one nearly reached her eyes. 'I'm actually quite good at it when I try.'

His conscience gave another gasp. He should have thought to check that she was settling in, but she had been so efficient from day one. *Besides*, the annoying ghost of conscience past whispered, *if you had noticed, what would you have done about it*? But she *had* put a lot of work in tonight and it *was* her birthday… Even Kit couldn't be so callous as to abandon her to a lonely night of pizza and a romcom. 'I can't possibly let you go home alone to watch a film on your birthday, especially after all the hard work you put in today. The least I can do is buy you a drink.' He looked at his blue drink and shuddered. 'A real drink. What do you say?'

CHAPTER TWO

SHE SHOULD HAVE said no.

The last thing Maddison needed was a pity date. Even worse, a pity date with her *boss*. But Kit had caught her at a vulnerable moment. Nice as it was to be flirted with by not just one, or two, but several men at the party, all of whom had their own teeth, hair and impressive-sounding job titles, she couldn't help but remember this time last year and the adorable little inn in Connecticut Bart had whisked her off to. Three months ago she was reasonably confident that this birthday he'd propose—not break up with her two months before.

Which meant she wouldn't be married at twenty-seven and a mother by twenty-eight. Her whole, carefully planned timetable redundant. Somehow she was going to have to start again. Only she had no idea how or who or where...

Happy birthday to me. Maddison sighed, the

age-long loneliness forcing its way out of the box she had buried it in, creeping back around her heart, her soul. It wasn't that she minded the lack of cards and presents. She'd got used to that a long time ago. But she couldn't help feeling that at twenty-six her birthday should matter to someone. Especially to her. Instead she'd been in denial all day. She wasn't sure why she'd mentioned it to the young sales guy, maybe some pathetic need to have some kind of acknowledgement, no matter how small.

That's enough. She wasn't a wallower, she was a fighter and she never, ever looked back. Maddison pushed herself off the plush velvet sofa and paced the length of the room. If she did have to wait in Kit Buchanan's house while he changed then she might as well take advantage and find out as much as she could about him. From the little she had gathered he was a constant source of speculation at work, but although the gossips were full of theories they had very few solid facts. A few juicy titbits could give her a way in with the social groups at work. She couldn't just bury herself and her sore pride away for the whole six months like some Roman exile marooned on a cold and damp island.

After all, the weather in London was much nicer than she had expected.

At least it was just her pride that hurt. She'd never be foolish enough to give away her heart without some kind of security.

Stop thinking about it, Maddison scolded herself, looking up at the high ceiling as if in supplication. She had five months left in London; she needed to start living again so she could return to New York full of European polish and fizzing with adventure. If that didn't bring Bart back on his knees, diamond ring in one hand, nothing would. After all, didn't they say absence made the heart grow fonder? Think how fond he could grow if word got back to him of just how good a time she was having in London...

A piece of elaborate-looking plaster work caught her eye. Original, she'd bet, just like the tiles on the hallway floor and the ceiling roses holding the anachronistically modern lights. The huge semi-detached house overlooking a lushly green square was the last place she'd expected Kit to live; she would have laid money on some kind of trendy apartment, all glass and chrome, not the white-painted Georgian house. It was even more impressive than Bart's brownstone.

She hadn't seen much in the way of personal touches so far. A tiled hallway with no clutter at all, just a hat stand, a mirror and an antique sideboard with a small bowl for his keys. There was nothing left lying around in the living room either except a newspaper on the coffee table, neatly folded at the nearly completed crossword, and just one small photo on the impressive marble mantle—a black-and-white picture of two teenage boys, grinning identical smiles, hanging over the rail on a boat. She had no trouble identifying the younger one as Kit, although there was something about the smile that struck her as different from the smile she knew. Maybe it was how wide, how unadulterated, how whole-hearted it was, so different from the cynically amused expression she saw every day.

The sound of footsteps on the stairs sent her scuttling back to her seat, where she grabbed the newspaper and scanned it, carefully giving the impression she had been comfortably occupied for the last ten minutes.

'Sorry to keep you. I spilled some of that green stuff on my shirt and didn't fancy going out smelling like the ghost of absinthe past.' Kit walked into the room and raised an eyebrow. Maddison had kicked off her shoes and was curled up in a corner of the sofa, the newspaper on her knee, looking as studiously un-detective-like as possible. 'Comfy?'

'Hmm? No, I was fine. Just finishing off your crossword. I think it's Medusa.'

'I beg your pardon?'

'Six down. *Petrifying snakes.* Medusa.'

'Here, give me that.' He took the paper off her and stared at the clue. 'Of course. I should have thought…' He looked back up and over at her, his eyes impossibly blue as they took her in.

'Do you like puzzles, Maddison?'

'I'm sorry?' It took all her resolution to stay still under such scrutiny. It was as if he were looking at her for the first time, as if he were weighing her up.

'Puzzles, quizzes? Do you like them?'

'Well, sure. Doesn't everyone?' He didn't reply, just stared at her in that disconcertingly intense way. 'I mean, when I was a kid I wanted to be Nancy Drew.' When she hadn't dreamed of being Rory Gilmore, that was. She swung her legs to the floor. 'I believe you mentioned a drink.'

He didn't move for a long second, his eyes still focused on her, and then smiled, the familiar amused expression sliding back on to his face like a mask. 'Of course. It's not far. I hope you don't mind the walk.'

Maddison hadn't known what to expect on a night out with Kit Buchanan: a glitzy wine bar or maybe some kind of private members' bar, all leather seats and braying, privileged laughter. She definitely hadn't expected the comfortable pub Kit guided her into. The walls were hung with prints by local artists, the tables solid square wood surrounded by leather sofas and chairs. It was nearly full but it didn't feel crowded or loud; it felt homely, like a pub from a book. The man behind the bar nodded at Kit and gave Maddison a speculative look as Kit guided her to a nook by the unlit fire before heading off to order their drinks.

'I got a sharing platter as well,' he said as he set the bottle of Prosecco on the table and placed a glass in front of her. 'I don't know about you but I'm starving. I never get a chance to eat at those work parties. It's hard to schmooze with a half-eaten filo prawn in my mouth.'

'When I started out in events sometimes canapés were all I did eat,' Maddison confessed, watching as he filled her glass up. 'New York is pricey for a girl out of college and free food is free food. Some days I would long for a good old-fashioned sub or a real-sized burger rather than an assortment of finger food! Turns out a girl can have too much caviar.'

'Happy birthday.' Kit handed her a glass before taking the seat opposite her, raising his glass to her. 'You worked in events?'

She nodded. 'After I graduated I joined a friend's PR and events company.' It had been the perfect job, working in the heart of Manhattan with the heart of society—until her friend had decided she preferred attending parties to planning them, being in the headlines rather than creating them. 'After that I landed a junior management role at DL Media and then Brenda poached me. I've only worked in editorial for the last six months,' she added. She still wasn't sure how Brenda had persuaded her to leave the safe world of PR for the unknown waters of editorial. It was the first unplanned move Maddison had made in a decade. It still terrified her, both the spontaneity and the starting again.

'Six months? I did wonder why you were still at an assistant level when you are obviously so capable.' The words were casually said but Maddison sat up a little straighter, pride swelling her chest.

She looked around the room, not wanting Kit to see just how the offhand praise had affected her. 'It's nice here. Is this where you bring all the girls?'

'You're the first.'

She turned and looked at him, laughter ready on her lips but there was no answering smile. He was serious. 'Consider me honoured. Why not? It's pretty convenient.'

Kit shrugged. 'I don't like to bring anyone home. It gives them ideas. One moment a cosy dinner, the next a sleepover and before you know it they're rearranging the furniture and suggesting a drawer. Besides, Camilla and her ilk only like to go to places where they can see and be seen. This place isn't anywhere near trendy enough for them.'

It sounded pretty lonely. Maddison knew all about that. 'So if you don't want to share your home or local with these girls, why date them?'

His eyes darkened for a stormy moment. 'Because I am in absolutely no danger of falling in love with any of them.'

He had said too much. This was supposed to be a casual 'thank you and by the way happy birthday' drink, not a full-on confessional. He didn't need or deserve absolution. Maddison stared at him, her eyes wide and mouth half-open as if he were some kind of crossword clue she could solve, and for once he couldn't think of the right kind of quip to turn her attention aside. He breathed a sigh of relief as the waitress came over, their Mediterranean platter balanced high on one hand, and broke the mounting tension.

'If I'd known you had overdosed on canapés I'd have ordered something more substantial,' he said, gesturing at the bowls of olives and sundried tomatoes, hummus and aioli. 'The bread's reasonably sized though.'

'No, this is good, thanks.' But she sounded thoughtful and her eyes were still fixed disturbingly on him. Kit searched for a change of subject.

'Have you heard from Hope?' That was safe enough.

Maddison speared a falafel and placed it delicately onto her plate, every movement precise, just as she was in the office. 'A couple of emails. I think she's settled in.' She smiled then, a completely unguarded, full-on smile, and Kit's chest twisted at the openness of it. 'She intimidates me a little. I thought I was organized, but Hope? She beats me every time. Did you know she left me a printed-out file, all alphabetized, with instructions on what to do if the boiler breaks and when the trash goes out? Half of it is about what I need to do if her sister, Faith, comes home early from her travels or phones or something. I mean, the girl's nineteen. Cut her some slack!' But although the words were mocking there was a wistfulness in Maddison's face that belied them.

She took a deep breath and her features recomposed until she was back to her usual calm and efficient self. 'Anyway, some of her neighbours have dropped round and been welcoming, which is very kind but they're older and have kids. They're nice but a night spent in talking about the cost of childcare isn't exactly something I can contribute to.'

Kit grimaced. 'No, I can empathize with that. It seems that every time I go out now someone is talking about nannies or the importance of organic baby food.' Each time it was a reminder that his friendship group was moving on without him, the teasing about his bachelor status beginning to grate.

She raised her eyes to his. 'Don't you want kids? One day?'

He laughed shortly. 'Why does it all come back to kids and marriage? I thought society had evolved beyond that. Why not just enjoy some company for a while and then move on?'

Maddison was frozen, her fork in her hand. 'That's really what you think? Poor Camilla.'

Kit frowned. 'She knew the score. I don't pretend to be anything different, to want anything different, Maddison. If she wants to change the rules without checking to see if I'm still playing along then that's not my problem.'

'People change. No one goes into a relationship expecting it to stay static. Relationships evolve. They grow or they end. It's the way it has to be.'

'I don't agree. It's perfectly possible for two people to enjoy themselves with no expectations of anything more. Look, Camilla said she was happy enough with a casual thing but it didn't take long before she started pushing for more. If she'd been more honest with herself, with me, at the beginning, then she wouldn't have got hurt.'

'Wow. You've actually made me feel a little sorry for her.' The colour was high on her cheeks and he opened his mouth to do what? Defend himself? No, to put her straight, but anything he might have said was drowned out as the pub's PA system crackled into life with an announcement of that night's quiz.

Maddison straightened and looked around, her eyes bright like a child promised a treat. 'Oh, I haven't done a quiz since college. Do you want to…? I mean, we've barely started on the wine and there's all that bread to eat.'

Interesting. Kit sat back and looked at her; she was practically fizzing with anticipation. His mind flashed back to the completed crossword, to the way she had meticulously sorted every single problem that had come his way for the last four weeks. *I wanted to be Nancy Drew,* she had said.

Could he trust her? It wasn't just that he didn't want any of his commercial rivals getting any hint of what he was up to; he didn't want it known internally either. He didn't want project-management groups and focus studies and sales input. That would come, but not yet. Not while he was enjoying the thrill of the new.

'Maddison,' he said slowly. 'How would you like to be my guinea pig?'

'Your *what*?' She couldn't have looked more outraged if he'd asked her if she wanted to eat a guinea pig.

'Guinea pig. Testing out my new product.'

Her eyes narrowed. 'How very marketing friendly of you. I was under the impression that we produced books.'

'Oh, we do. I do.' He considered her for a moment longer. She didn't really know anyone to tell and didn't strike him as the gossiping type anyway. He should trust her. He hadn't come this far without taking some risks.

Kit had started his publishing career while still at Cambridge, republishing forgotten golden-age crime books for a nostalgic audience. Two years later he'd diversified into digital genre publishing before selling his company to DL Media for a tidy sum and an executive position. The sale had paid for his house and furnished him with a nice disposable income and a nest egg, but lately he'd been wondering if he'd sold his soul, not just his company.

He had had no idea just how different things would be. The sole guy in charge of a small but growing company was a million miles away from a cog in a huge international corporation— even an executive cog. And although the perks and salary were nice—more than nice—he missed the adrenaline rush of ownership. This project was making his blood pump in almost the same way as building up his imprint had. While he was working on it he almost forgot everything else that had changed in the last few years.

Maddison's eyes were fixed on his face. 'So what is this product?'

Kit watched her every reaction. 'Okay, so we

produce entertainment and information. I am planning to marry the two together.'

Maddison frowned. 'And you want me to bless the happy couple?'

'I want you to road-test them.' He took a deep breath. He was going in. 'I'm planning a series of new interactive guidebooks.'

'Okay…' Scepticism was written all over her face. 'That's interesting but does anyone even use guidebooks any more?'

Kit had been expecting that. 'Guidebooks available in every format from eBook to app to good old-fashioned paper copies.'

'I still don't see…'

He took pity on her. 'The difference is that they don't tell you what to see, they give you clues. Each guidebook is a treasure hunt.'

She leaned forward, a spark of interest lighting up her face, transforming her from merely pretty to glowingly beautiful. Not that Kit was interested in her looks. It was her brains he was after; he was certainly not focusing on how her eyes lit up when she was engaged or the way her blouse dipped a little lower as she shifted forward. 'A treasure hunt? As in X marks the spot?'

He tore his eyes away from her mouth. *Focus, Buchanan.* 'In a way. Tourists can pick from one of five or so themed routes—historical, romantic, wild, fictional or a mixture of all the themes and follow a series of clues to their mystery destination, taking in places of interest on the way. Each theme will have routes of varying length ranging from an afternoon to three days, allowing people to adapt the treasure hunt to their length of stay, although I very much hope even cynical Londoners will want to have a go.'

'Yes.' She nodded slowly, her still-half-full plate pushed to one side as she took in every word. 'I see, each hunt would have a unique theme depending on the place like, I don't know, say a revolution theme in Boston? It wouldn't just be tourists, though, would it? I mean, something like this would work for team building, bachelor and bachelorette parties, family days out…' Satisfaction punched through him. She'd got it. 'And what's the prize—or is taking part enough?'

'Hopefully the satisfaction of a job well done, but successful treasure hunters will also be able to pick up some discounts for local restaurants and attractions. I'm looking into building some partnerships. To launch it, however, I am planning real treasure—or a prize at least.'

Maddison leaned back and picked up her wine glass. 'And you want me to what? Source the prize for you?'

Kit shook his head. 'No, I want you to test the first few routes. The plan is to launch next year, simultaneously in five cities around the world. Each launch will open up on the same day and teams will compete against each other. But for now, in order to present a full proposal to marketing, we've been concentrating on drawing up the London routes—and I want to know how hard it is, especially to non-Brits, if the timings work and, crucially, if it's fun.'

'So, this will be part of my job?'

Kit picked up his own glass; he was about to ask a lot from her. 'We're still very much in concept stage at the moment. This would be in your own time at weekends. But…' he smiled directly at her, turning up the charm '…you said yourself you needed to get out and about…'

'I didn't say that at all. For all you know I am completely happy with takeaways and box sets.

Maybe that's the whole reason I took this job,' she protested.

He watched her carefully, looking for an advantage. 'But you're spending your weekends alone. I know the routes but not the clues so I want to see how it works in practice. I was going to go around on my own but here you are, new to London. A non-Brit. It's perfect. You can follow the clues and I'll accompany you and see how it works.'

'I…'

'I don't expect you to do it for nothing,' he broke in before she talked herself out of it or pointed out that spending every weekend with her boss was not her idea of fun. 'Each route we complete has a prize. An experience of your choice, fully paid. Gigs, concerts, theme parks, restaurants—you name it.'

'Anything I want?'

'Anything.' Now where had that come from? He would be spending all week and most of the next few weekends with her, did he really want to add in leisure time as well? But before he could backtrack Maddison held out her hand.

'In that case you have a deal,' she said.

In for a penny… He took her soft, cool hand in his. 'Deal. I'm looking forward to getting to know you better.'

Why had he said that? That wasn't part of the deal. So she was proving to be a bit of an enigma, a girl who liked a challenge? They were reasons to stay away, not get closer. But this was purely business and business Kit could handle. It was all he had left, after all.

CHAPTER THREE

ALTHOUGH CLISSOLD PARK couldn't hold a candle to her own beloved Central Park, the small London park had a quirky charm all its own. There might not be a fairy-tale castle or boats for hire on the little duck-covered lakes, but it was always buzzing with people and a circuit made for a pretty run.

Maddison increased her pace, smiling as she overtook a man pushing a baby in a jogger. Not so much difference between Clissold and Central Parks after all—and yes, right on cue, there it was: a t'ai chi ch'uan class. City parks were city parks no matter their location and size.

The biggest difference was that dogs roamed unleashed and free through the London park; in Central Park they would be allowed to walk untethered only in the doggy-exercise areas. Maddison nervously eyed a large, barrel-chested brown dog hurtling towards her, the sweat springing onto her palms nothing to do with the exercise. Could it smell her fear? She wavered, torn between increasing her pace and stopping to back away from it when it jumped, running directly... past her to retrieve a ball, slobber flying from its huge jowls. Maddison's heart hammered and she gulped in some much-needed air. She hated dogs; they were unpredictable. She'd found that out the hard way—and had the scar on her thigh to prove it. At least her mom had dumped that particular boyfriend after his dog had attacked Maddison, but whether it was the dog bite that had precipitated the move or some other misdemeanour Maddison had never known.

Maddison increased the pace again, the pain in her chest and the ache in her thighs a welcome distraction from thoughts of the past—and the immediate future. In one hour Kit Buchanan would be knocking on her door and she would be spending the whole day with him. Whatever had possessed her to agree?

On the other hand she didn't have anything better to do. And despite her reservations she had had fun last night. For the first time in a long time she had been able to relax, to be her-

self. She only needed to impress Kit professionally; what he made of her socially wasn't at all
important.

It was a long time since she hadn't had to
worry about that.

Maddison turned out of the park and began
to run along the pavement, dodging the myriad
small tables cluttering up the narrow pavements
outside the many cafes and coffee shops that
made up the main street, until she reached the
small road where she was staying. Her stomach
twisted as she opened the front door and stepped
over the threshold, the heaviness in her chest
nothing to do with the exercise.

Try as she might to ignore it, staying in Hope's
old family home was opening up old wounds, allowing the loneliness to seep through. It wasn't
the actual living alone—apart from the semes-
ters sleeping in her college dorm Maddison had
lived by herself since she was sixteen. No, she
thought that this unshakeable melancholy was
because Hope's home was, well, a home. A
much-loved family home with the family photos
clustered on the dresser downstairs, the battered
kitchen table, the scuff marks in the hallway

where a generation of shoes had been kicked off to prove it.

And sure, Maddison wouldn't have picked the violet-covered wallpaper and matching purple curtains and bedspread in her room, just as she would have stripped the whole downstairs back for a fresh white and wood open-plan finish, but she appreciated why Hope had preserved the house just the way it must have been when her parents died. There was love in every in-need-of-a-refresh corner.

Losing her parents so young must have been hard but at least Hope had grown up with them, in a house full of light and happiness.

Maddison's childhood bedroom had no natural light and pretty near little happiness. The thin bunks and thinner walls, the sound of the TV blaring in if she was lucky, silence if she wasn't. If she was alone. It was only temporary, her mother reassured her, just somewhere to stay until their luck changed.

Only it never did. That was when Maddison stopped believing in luck. That was when she knew it was down to her, only her.

Maddison found herself, as she often did, looking at the photos displayed on the hallway side-board. Both girls were slim with dark hair and dark eyes but whereas Hope looked perpetually worried and careworn, Faith sparkled with vital-ity. Reading between the lines of Hope's com-prehensive file, Maddison got the impression that the older sister was the adult in this house, the younger protected and indulged. But Faith was nineteen! At that age Maddison had been on her own for three years and was putting her-self through college, the luxury of a year spent travelling as remote as her chances of discover-ing a secret trust fund.

Maddison picked up her favourite photo. It was taken when their parents were still alive; the whole family were grouped on a beach at sunset, dressed in smart summery clothes. Faith must have been around six, a small, merry-faced imp with laughing eyes and a naughty smile, holding hands with her mother. Hope, a teenager all in black, was standing in front of her father, casual in his arms. She was probably at the age where she was so secure in her parents' love and affec-tion she took it for granted, embarrassed by any public show. It used to make Maddison mad to

see how casually her schoolmates treated their
parents, how dismissive they could be of their
love.

One day Maddison wanted a photo like this.
She and her own reliable, affectionate husband
and their secure, happy children. A family of
her own. It wasn't too much to ask, was it? She'd
thought she was so close with Bart and now here
she was. As far away as ever. The heaviness in
her chest increased until she wanted to sink to
her knees under the burden.

Stop it, she told herself fiercely. Kit would be
here soon and she still had to shower and change.
Besides, what good had feeling sorry for herself ever done? Planning worked. Timetables
worked. Things didn't just happen because you
wished for them or were good. You had to make
your own destiny.

It didn't take Maddison long to get ready or
to post a few pictures of her evening's adventures onto her various social-media accounts,
captioning them 'Birthday in London'—and if
they were carefully edited to give the impression that she was a guest at the party, not work-

ing, and that there was a whole group at the pub, well, wasn't social media all about perception?

Her phone flashed with notifications and Maddison quickly scrolled through them. It was funny to see life carrying on in New York as if she hadn't left: the same parties, the same hook-ups and break-ups. She chewed her lip as she scrolled through another Friday night of cocktails, exclusive clubs and VIP bars. At least her bank balance was healthier during her London exile. Keeping up with the Trustafarians without a trust fund was a constant balancing act. One she was never in full control of. Thank goodness she had landed a rent-controlled apartment.

Still, she had to speculate to accumulate and if Maddison wanted the security of an Upper East Side scion with the houses, bank balance and guaranteed happy life to match, then she needed to make some sacrifices. And she didn't just want that security, she needed it. She knew too well what the alternatives were and she had no intention of ever being that cold, that hungry, that despised ever again.

The sound of the doorbell snapped her back to reality. She stood, breathing in, trying to squash the old fears, the old feelings of inadequacy, the knowledge that she would never be good enough, back into the little box she hid them in. She should have learned from Pandora; some things were better left locked away.

The doorbell sounded again before she made it downstairs and she wrenched the front door open to find Kit leaning against the door frame, looking disturbingly casual in faded jeans and a faded red T-shirt. Morning. Recovered from your victory yet?'

Maddison felt the heat steal over her cheeks. Maybe it hadn't been the most dignified thing in the world to fling her arms up in the air and whoop when she and Kit were declared pub-quiz champions but it *had* been her birthday. And they had won pretty darn convincingly. 'Are you kidding? I want a certificate framed for my wall so I can show it to my grandkids in forty years' time.'

She grabbed her bag and stepped out, pulling the door shut behind her.

Kit waited while she double-and then triple-locked the door as per Hope's comprehensive instructions. 'Right. As I mentioned yesterday we need to keep things as simple as possible. The idea is to give people a fun and unique way of seeing London, not to bamboozle them completely. Plus our target market is going to be tourists, the vast majority of whom aren't English, so we need to make this culturally accessible to everyone whether it's a girl from New York…' he smiled at Maddison '…or a family from China or a couple from France.'

'More of a scavenger hunt than a treasure hunt?'

'A mix of the two. Every destination is accessible by Tube or bus to make it easier, at least to start with, and we're putting the nearest stop with each clue with directions from that stop. On the app and on the online version you won't get the next clue until you put in an answer for the current quest but that would be impossible on paper. The discounts you get will be linked to how many correct answers you have in the end.'

'And what's to stop people going online and cheating?'

'Eventually? Nothing. But hopefully the fun of the quest will stop them wanting to find shortcuts. And the discounts will be the kind you get with most standard tourist passes so nice to have but not worth cheating for.'

'Have you thought about randomizing it? You know, every fifth hundred correct—or completed—quest gets something extra? Just to add that bit more spice into it.'

'No.' He stared at her. 'But that's a great idea. I'll plan that in. Good thinking, Maddison.'

'Just doing my job.' But that same swell of pride flared up again. 'So, what's the plan? Where are we starting off? Literary? History?'

Kit held up a map and grinned. 'Neither. How do you feel about seeing the wild side of London?'

'When you said wild…' Maddison stood still on the path and stared '…I thought you meant the zoo!'

'Nope.' Kit shook his head solemnly but his eyes were shining with suppressed laughter. He seemed more relaxed, more boyish out and about. It was almost relaxing. But last night's words beat a warning tattoo through her head. There was a darkness at the heart of him and she needed to make sure she wasn't blinded by the veneer.

Not that she was attracted to Kit. Obviously not. A handsome face and a keen brain might be enough to turn some girls' heads but she was made of stronger stuff. No being led astray by blue eyes and snug-fitting jeans for Maddison, no allowing the odd spark of attraction to flare into anything hotter. Think first, feel after, that was her motto.

Speaking of which, she was here to think. Maddison looked around. She was used to city parks—Central Park was her gym, garden, playground and sanctuary—but the sheer number of green spaces on the map Kit held loosely in one hand had taken her aback. London was surprisingly awash in nature reserves, parks, heaths, woods and cemeteries. Yes, cemeteries. Like the one lying before her, for instance. Winding paths, crumbling mausoleums and trees, branches entwining over the paths as they bent to meet each other like lovers refusing to be separated even by death. Maddison put one hand onto the wrought-iron gate and raised a speculative eyebrow. 'Seriously? You're sending people to graveyards? For fun?'

'This is one of London's most famous spots,' Kit said as he led the way through the gates and into the ancient resting place. Maddison hesitated for a moment before following him in. It was like entering another world. She had to admit it was surprisingly peaceful in a gloomy, gothic kind of way. Birds sang in the trees overhead and the early-summer sun did its valiant best to peep through the branches and cast some light onto the grey stone fashioned into simple headstones, huge mausoleums and twisted, crumbling statues. 'There's a fabulous Victorian cemetery near you in Stoke Newington too but there's no Tube link so I didn't include it in the tour.'

'You can save it for the future, a grave tour of London.'

'I could.' She couldn't tell whether he was ignoring her sarcasm or taking her seriously. 'There are seven great Victorian cemeteries, all fantastic in different ways. But I love disused ones best, watching nature reclaim them, real dust-to-dust, ashes-to-ashes stuff.'

'Don't tell me.' She stopped still and put her
hands on her hips. 'You wore all black as a
teenager and had a picture of Jim Morrison on
your wall? Wrote bitter poetry about how nobody understood you and went vegetarian for
six months.'

'Naturally. Doesn't every wannabe creative?
You forgot learning two chords on a guitar and
refusing to smile. Does that sum up your teen
years too?'

It certainly hadn't. She hadn't had the luxury.
People didn't like their waitresses, babysitters,
baristas and cleaners to be anything but perky
and wholesome. Especially when their hired
help had a background like Maddison's. She'd
had to be squeaky clean in every single way.
The quintessential all-American girl, happy to
help no matter how demanding her customer,
demeaning the job and low the pay.

'Not my bag,' she said airily. 'I like colour,
light and optimism.'

Kit grinned and began to pick his way along
the path. On either side mausoleums, gravestones and crumbling statues, some decorated
with fading flowers, formed a curious hon-

our guard. 'What was your bag? Let me guess: cheerleader?'

Maddison tossed her hair back. 'Possibly.'

'Mall rat?'

'I would say Mall Queen,' she corrected him.

'Daddy's credit card, a cute convertible and Homecoming Queen?'

'Were you spying on me?' she countered. Actually it had been a rusty bike she had saved up for herself and then repaired. Not a thing of beauty but she had been grateful at the time.

He fell into step beside her, an easy lope to his stride. Her brightly patterned skirt, her neat little cashmere cardigan and elegant brogues were too bright, too alive for this hushed, grey and green world and yet Kit fitted right in, despite his casual jeans. He belonged. 'So where did you spend your cheerleading years?'

'You wouldn't have heard of it. It's just a typical New England small town.' Maddison was always careful not to get too drawn into details; that was how a girl got caught out. She didn't want anyone to know the sordid truth. She much preferred the fiction. The life she wished she had led. So she kept the generalities the same and the details vague. 'How about you? Have you always lived in London?'

He looked surprised at her question. 'No, I'm from Kilcanon. It's by the sea, on the coast south of Glasgow on a peninsula between the mainland and the islands. Scotland,' he clarified as she frowned.

'You're Scottish?' How had she not known that?

'You can't tell?'

'You don't sound Scottish, you sound British!'

He laughed. 'We don't all sound like Groundskeeper Willie, well, not all the time.'

'Do you miss it?' She only had the haziest idea about Scotland, mostly bare-chested men in kilts and romantic countryside. It sounded pretty good; maybe she should pay it a visit.

'Every day,' he said so softly she almost couldn't hear the words. 'But this is where I live now.'

'I love living in New York but I wouldn't want to raise my children there.'

'Children?' He raised his eyebrows. 'How many are you planning?'

'Four,' she said promptly. 'Two girls, two boys.'

His mouth quirked into a half-smile. 'Naturally. Do they have names?'

'Anne, Gilbert, Diana and Matthew. This week anyway. It depends on what I've been reading.' Actually it was always those names. They gave her hope. After all, didn't Anne Shirley start off with nothing and yet end up surrounded by laughter and love?

'Let's hope you're not on a sci-fi kick when you're actually pregnant then, or your kids could end up with some interesting names. Why so many?'

'Sorry?'

'Four children. That's a lot of kids to transport around. You'll need a big car, a big house—a huge washing machine.'

'I'm an only child,' she said quietly. That, for once, wasn't a prevarication, not a stretch of the truth. And she had vowed that when she got her family, when she had kids, then everything would be different. They would be wanted, loved, praised, supported—and they would have each other. There would be no lonely nights shivering under a thin comforter and wishing that there were just one person to share it with her. One person who understood. 'It gets kind of lonely. I want my children to have the most perfect childhood ever.'

The childhood she was meant to have had. The one she had been robbed of when her mother refused to name her father. All she had said was that he was a summer visitor. One of the golden tribe who breezed into town in expensive cars with boats and designer shades and lavish tips. Maddison could have been one of them, but instead she had been the trailer-trash daughter of an alcoholic mother. No gold, just tarnish so thick hardly anyone saw through it to the girl within. Even when she had got out, the tarnish had still clung—until she left the Cape altogether and reinvented herself.

Kit looked directly at her as she spoke, as if he could see through to the heart of her. But he couldn't; no one could. She had made sure of that. And yet her pulse sped up under his gaze, hammering so loudly she could almost hear the beat reverberate through the cemetery. She cast about for a change of subject.

'How about you? Do you have any brothers and sisters besides Bridget?'

Kit wandered over to a statue of a lichen-covered dog waiting patiently for eternity. Maddison shivered a little, relieved of the warmth of his gaze, pulling her cardigan a little tighter around her. 'There were three of us.'

Were?

Her unspoken question hung in the air. 'My sister's a lot younger, she's still at university, but my brother...he died. Three years ago.'

'I'm sorry,' she said softly. 'You must miss him.'

He turned, his smile not reaching his eyes. 'Every day. Okay, where are we headed?'

Maddison swallowed. It was a clear change of subject. He was not going to discuss his loss with her. There was no reason why he should; they barely knew each other. And yet there had been a connection last night, and now as they wandered through the gravestones. Maybe she'd imagined it. After all, didn't she know how powerful imagination was? How important.

She held up the piece of paper and read out the first clue once again. '"Take the Northern line to Archway. Walk up Highgate Hill and through Waterlow Park to the final resting place of the city. Unite at the grave where you have nothing to lose but your chains. The last words on the fourth line are…?"' She paused and looked up at Kit. 'Unite at the grave? What does that mean? We have to split up?'

'See, this is where in the actual trail you'll read the information about Highgate Cemetery in the guidebook and hopefully work the clue out from there. Here.' He passed her his phone. 'Read that.'

She took it carefully and squinted down at the screen, angling it away from the sun so that she could make out the words. '"Famous people buried here include Douglas Adams, George Eliot and Christina Rossetti, although many people bypass even these luminaries and head straight to the grave of Karl Marx…" Oh! Of course.' She read through the rest of the list. 'Lizzie Siddal's buried here too? I'd love to see her grave. I did a paper on the Pre-Raphaelites at college.'

'Take your time. The whole point of this is that it's fun and a way to explore London, not to tear around like some kind of city-wide scavenger hunt.'

'True, but I'm testing it, not doing it for real,'

she pointed out. 'I can come back. I might even explore the one in Stoke Newington. Maybe you've converted me to gothic tourism.'

'That's the aim. I'll get you on to a Ripper tour yet. Look, there's a tour guide. Why don't you ask him the way?'

'Only if you take my photo when we get there.' Maddison examined the picture of the grave in fascination. 'I've seen a lot of hipster beards since I got to London but Karl Marx has them all beat. I want to capture that for posterity.' It wasn't quite the type of picture she had intended to fill her social-media sites with but hey. Let Bart see she had hidden depths.

And more importantly that she was out, about and having fun.

Only, Maddison reflected as she walked towards the guide to ask for directions, it wasn't all for show. She probably wouldn't have chosen to spend her weekend in this way but she *was* having fun. And even more oddly, until the last minute she hadn't thought about Bart once all morning.

She'd been banking on absence making the heart grow fonder but in her case it seemed that out of sight really was out of mind. Well, good. Maddison Carter didn't hang around weeping about any guy, no matter how perfect he was. And the more she made that clear, the more likely he would be banging on her door the second she got back to New York, begging for a second chance.

That was the plan, wasn't it? But the image didn't have its usual uplifting effect and for the first time Maddison couldn't help wondering that if she had to go to such extraordinary efforts to persuade Bart that she was the girl for him then maybe, just maybe, he wasn't the guy for her.

And if he wasn't, then she had no idea what to do next.

CHAPTER FOUR

'WHAT HAVE YOU got planned for me today?'
Maddison looked up at the threatening-looking
sky and wrinkled her nose. 'And what did you
do with the sunshine?'

'I forgot to order it.' Kit gestured towards the
end of the street. 'Shall we?'

'Okay, but there better be more transport today
because, I am warning you, my feet are planning
on going on strike after two miles.'

He wasn't surprised by her declaration. They
had covered a huge amount of distance the day
before, walking to Hampstead Heath from Highgate where, after deciphering the clue, Maddison
had found out the opening times of the famous
all-season open-air pool. From there they had
travelled to first Regent's and then Hyde Park
before searching for Peter Pan's statue in Ken-
sington Gardens. Less a leisurely treasure hunt,
more a route march through London's parks.

And Maddison hadn't complained once.

She had turned all his preconceptions on their head this weekend. She had surprised him, shamed him a little, with the speech she had produced, with her sharp criticism of his own effort. Charmed him with her unabashed competitiveness in the pub quiz; and yesterday she had unflaggingly followed the clues, suggesting improvements and possible new additions. Not once had she moaned about sore feet or tried to steer him into a shop. He tried to imagine Camilla under similar circumstances and suppressed a smile. Unless her treasure hunt took her down Bond Street she was likely to give up at the first clue.

What was he doing with women like Camilla? He'd thought he was choosing wisely, safely, but maybe he would be better off on his own. It was what he deserved, after all. Although sometimes his dating habits seemed like some eternal punishment, his own personal Hades.

Maddison stopped. 'The bus stop is just here. I was a bit horrified when I realized I was going to have to bus in to work but actually I love that I spend every day on a real red double-decker.

It's like an adventure. I never quite know where it might take me.'

Kit's mouth curled into a reluctant smile, his bitter thoughts banished by her enthusiasm. Turned out Maddison Carter had quite the imagination. 'Doesn't it stop at the bus stop outside work?'

'Well, yeah, that's where I choose to get off. But sometimes I wonder if it might turn an unexpected corner and poof. There I am, in Victorian London, or Tudor London. Even in New York I don't feel that. Oh, we have some wonderful old houses back home but they're babies compared to some of the buildings I see here.'

'We'll have to do the history tour next. That will blow your mind.' The bus pulled in at that moment and they got on, tapping their cards on the machine by the driver before ascending the narrow, twisting staircase to the top deck. Yesterday was the first time Kit had been on a bus in a really long time, and personally he was struggling to see any hint of adventure travelling in the slow, crowded vehicle, but to test the routes properly he needed to travel the way his intended market would. However long it took.

He would taxi home though; that wouldn't be cheating.

The bus lurched forward as he slid into a narrow seat beside Maddison. She was wearing the same brightly patterned skirt as yesterday teamed with another neat cashmere cardigan, this one in a bright blue that emphasized the red tones in her hair. She looked like a bird of paradise, far too elegant for the top deck of a bus—or a hike through a park. She had turned away to stare out the window, no doubt daydreaming of time-travelling adventures as the bus progressed slowly down a narrow street, stopping every few hundred yards to allow passengers on and off.

It was a good thing they had all day.

Kit shifted in his seat, trying to arrange his legs comfortably. 'Did you have a nice evening? A date with one of your conquests from the party?' Whatever she had done it had to have been better than his evening, an engagement party for an old friend. Camilla had been there, all quivering emotion and hurt eyes, his attempt to speak rationally to her thwarted by tears. It was funny, he thought grimly, how he had stuck to his word and yet somehow ended up the villain of the piece. At least she finally seemed to have accepted that they were over, had been over for some weeks and, no, he wasn't going to change his mind.

'A date?' Maddison turned and stared at him. 'I only met those men on Friday. It would be a bit early for me to accept a date off any of them even if they did ask me.'

Kit grinned at the indignation in her voice. 'Oh, I'm sorry. Do you need references and to meet the parents first?'

She didn't smile back, her face serious. 'No, but you never accept an invitation to a same-weekend date. Especially not for a first date.'

'You don't? How very unspontaneous.'

'Of course not.' She was sounding confused now. 'A girl needs to make sure any potential guy understands that she's a busy person, that she won't just drop everything for them.'

Kit frowned. 'But what if you don't have plans? What if you're turning down a night out for a box set and a takeaway?'

'It doesn't matter. If he doesn't respect you enough to try and book you in advance then he never will. You'll be relegated to a last-minute hook-up and once you're there you never move on.' Maddison turned to him, her eyes alight with curiosity. 'Isn't it like this in London?'

'I don't think so. Not that I've ever noticed. I say, "Want to grab a drink?" They say yes. Simple.' Simple at first, anyway.

'Or no. Surely sometimes they say no.'

Kit paused. 'Maybe.' But the truth was they usually said yes.

'Wow.' Maddison looked around as if answers were to be found somewhere on the bus. 'There's more than just an ocean between us, huh? Guess I'll never get a date in London. Or I'll end up civilizing your whole dating scene. Grateful women will build statues to me.'

The women Kit knew played enough mind games without adding some more to their repertoires. 'Remind me never to talk to a woman of dating age in New York again; I shudder to think of all the rules I must have inadvertently broken.' Although it must make life a little clearer, all these rules. It never failed to catch him unawares how quickly it could escalate—a coffee here, a drink there and suddenly there were expectations.

He suppressed a grin at Maddison's appalled face and couldn't resist shocking her a little more. 'If you want to meet someone in London then you need to be a lot less rigid. Over here we meet someone, usually in the pub, fancy them, don't know what to say to them, drink too much, kiss them, send some mildly flirty texts and panic that they'll be misconstrued and repeat until you're officially a couple.'

Maddison stared at him suspiciously. 'That's romantic.'

'You've seen *Four Weddings and a Funeral*, right? Think about it. If Andie MacDowell had understood the British Way of Dating she would never have married the other man, she would have just made sure she turned up at Hugh Grant's local pub a couple of times and that would be that.'

'Four Weddings, Three Nights Out and a Funeral?'

'That's it. Now you're ready to go. If you're looking, that is—or is there someone with the perfect dating etiquette waiting for you back in New York?'

'We're on a break.' The words were airily said

but, glancing at her, Kit was surprised to see a melancholy tint to her expression. Sadness mixed with something that looked a lot like fear.

'Because you came here?'

'Not really.' She shook her head, a small embarrassed laugh escaping her. 'I can't believe I'm telling you this.'

'I don't mind.'

Maddison paused, as if she were weighing up whether to carry on. 'Rule number two of dating,' she said eventually. 'Don't talk about your other relationships. Always seem mysterious and desirable at all times. Remember, rejected goods are never as attractive. Rules are rules, even when you're talking to your boss!'

'Your way sounds like a lot of hard work.' Kit stole a glance at her. Her face was pale, all the vibrant colour bleached out of it. He had been subjected to tears, tempers and sulks by his exes, often all three at once, and remained totally unmoved, but Maddison's stillness tugged at him. He wanted to see the warmth return to her expression; after all, he knew all about pain and regret, what a burden it was, how it infected everything. 'Look, if you want to talk about it forget I'm your boss. I've got a sister, remember? Sometimes I think she uses me as her very own Dear Diary.'

Maddison slid a long look up at him and Kit tried to look as confide-worthy as possible. It wasn't curiosity, not exactly. He just got the impression that she didn't let things out very often. Didn't allow her vulnerabilities to show. 'Rule number three, never assume you're exclusive, not until it's been formalized.' She sighed. 'I didn't assume but I let myself believe it was imminent. That he was in it for the long-term.'

'And you were? In it for the long-term?'

She nodded. 'When I first met him, right then, before we even spoke, before we had coffee or went for a walk or kissed. When I first met him I looked at him and I knew. Knew that I could grow old with him.'

Kit blinked. 'Like love at first sight?' He couldn't keep the scepticism out of his voice.

'No.' She shook her head, strawberry-blonde tendrils shaking with the motion. 'Not love. But compatibility, you know? That would grow into love? Two old people rocking on their porch at the end of a long day.'

'You got all that before hello?'

'The way he was standing, his hair, the cut of his suit. It said he was…' She paused, looking up at the bus roof as if for inspiration. 'He just looked like the way I always imagined my future to look. Does that make any sense at all? Have you never thought that way? That you could grow old with someone?'

Kit hesitated. 'Once,' he admitted reluctantly. 'But not straight away.' But the words didn't quite ring true. The reality was that right from the start he had been so dazzled by the image Eleanor portrayed that he had failed to look beneath the carefully applied gloss to the woman underneath.

'What happened?'

Kit tried to smile, as if it were nothing, but he knew all too well that it looked like a grimace. 'She married my brother.'

Maddison opened her mouth then shut it again. He understood that. What was there to say, after all? Kit pulled his phone out of his pocket and busied himself looking at emails. The subject was closed—it should never have been open at all.

Half an hour and a Tube train later they alighted at Notting Hill. He had been careful not to catch her eye, to start another conversation, knowing one more careless confession would shatter everything he worked so hard to contain. But they were here now and the game was back on. And so must he be. He switched on his usual smile, the one that was barely skin-deep.

'Ready?' Kit handed Maddison the first clue and, with one sweeping, comprehensive look at him, she took it. His message had been received and understood.

'"Turn left out of the station until you reach Holland Walk. What is Henry's man doing outside the place where East meets West and the Dutch play?"' she read aloud. 'How international. Are we still doing wild London?'

'Just for today.' After this he was planning south to the Chelsea Physic Garden and then east to Greenwich Park. Next weekend he was hoping that they could do the historical tour and literary the week after that—and then he would have enough data to put together a full proposal and Maddison could have her weekends back again.

As could he. The usual long, lonely weekends unless he buried himself with work or left London for two days of something outdoors, strenuous and a little dangerous.

Maddison repeated the clue to herself as they walked up the tree-lined splendour of Holland Park Avenue, past the white-painted, ornately decorated houses of this most exclusive of areas, breathing in a deep satisfied sigh as they turned into the park. 'I do love the countryside.'

Kit grinned. 'This isn't countryside, city girl. Two minutes that way and you're back in the heart of the city.' He stared unseeingly at the nearest tree. 'Back home there's nothing *but* trees and grass, water and mountains. The nearest supermarket's an hour's drive away on single-track roads, nothing remotely urban for miles around.'

'Sounds remote.'

'Yes.' He closed his eyes and pictured Kilcanon on a perfect day, the evening drawing in over the water, the vibrant greens fading to grey. Like Odysseus sitting on Circe's island, he felt a sudden piercing longing for his home. But unlike Odysseus there would be no happy homecoming at the end of his journey. His exile was self-imposed, necessary—and permanent. 'It's like no place on earth. But this is my home now, there's no going back. Not for me.'

And just like that he closed down, just as he had on the bus, and Maddison had no idea how to reach him—or even whether she should try. After all, they weren't friends, were they? They worked together, that was all.

But she didn't like to see anyone in pain and the darkness had returned, his eyes more navy than blue, his lips compressed as if he were holding all the emotions in the world tightly within.

'Because of your ex? And your brother?' The conversation from the graveyard yesterday returned to her and she stopped still, shock reverberating through her as she put the clues together. 'Wait, she married your brother, who died?' She regretted the words the second they snapped out of her mouth; there must have been a more sensitive way to have put it.

'Yes.'

'I'm sorry. For both.'

'Thank you.' They began to wander along the

path, following the signs to the Japanese garden, Maddison mentally ticking off part of the clue as she went.

'It can't have been easy for you.' And that, she thought with a grimace, was the understatement of the century.

His mouth twisted. 'I accepted long ago that the Eleanor I thought I was in love with doesn't exist. I just wish I had really been able to forgive Euan while I still could. I said I had, of course, but I never did. Not because she chose him over me. But because *he* chose *her* over me.' His mouth snapped shut and he marched along the path as if, like the White Rabbit, they were late.

Maddison walked slowly behind, giving Kit the space he needed. She didn't know a lot about families but she understood betrayal, knew that the worst wounds were inflicted by those who should put you first. No wonder he wasted his time with women who were safe, women he would never allow in too deep.

But his wounds were festering. When had he said his brother had died? Three years ago?

And he still hadn't dealt. If she didn't push now, maybe he never would.

But there were dangers in confidences. That was how bonds were formed, friendships forged. She should know; she'd honed her listening skills a long time ago—the right questions, a sympathetic face. She knew the drill. Used it to navigate her way into the right groups, the right cliques, the right life.

But this time she could use her skills for good. To help.

Darn altruism. She didn't have the time or space for it.

She stood, teetering on her decision. Flip the conversation back to clues and parks and grisly tours or probe deeper. She knew which was sensible...

Kit was standing by the entrance to the Japanese garden, a scruffy silhouette, hands in pockets. Maddison picked up her pace and closed the distance between them, mind made up. Light, frivolous words prepared. Only: 'Were you close?' fell from her lips instead.

He turned his head to look at her, his eyes distant, granite-like in their bleakness. Maddison stepped back, the shock almost physical. Gone was the annoying, teasing boss, gone her focused if entertaining weekend companion, in his place a hard-faced stranger reeking of grief.

'Once.'

'Until Eleanor?'

'Until Eleanor.' He walked into the garden, Maddison following, taking a moment to admire the deep oranges and reds in the expertly arranged planting perfectly setting off the delicate waterfalls and sculptures. She joined Kit on the wide stone bridge and stood by him, looking at the koi as they swam in the pond.

'She was everything I didn't know I wanted.'

Maddison's heart twisted at the words. Wasn't that what she aimed to be? Hadn't she tried to learn Bart? To be everything he didn't know he wanted? But her intentions were more honourable; if he wanted her, offered her the security she craved, she would look after his heart as if it were her own, do her very best to give him hers. Not break him into pieces.

'We were close, Euan and I. There's barely a year and a half between us and he was the oldest—he never let me forget that. But he had asthma and it held him back sometimes and I, I didn't let him forget that.'

He paused, still staring into the pond as if the koi carp could give him the answers she couldn't. But like her they just listened.

'I was in my last year at Cambridge when I brought Eleanor home. I'd never brought a girl back before. I couldn't wait for my family to meet her. But he couldn't help himself, couldn't help making even her into a competition and this time he won. How was I supposed to forgive him for that?'

Without thinking Maddison reached across the carefully maintained space between them and laid a hand on Kit's arm. It was firm, as she'd known it would be, warm. She wanted to leave her hand there, flesh on flesh, to allow her fingers to slip down the muscled forearm, to link around his wrist. Her heart began to hammer, every millimetre of her uncomfortably aware of his proximity, of the feel of him under her suddenly unsteady hand.

She had never experienced a visceral reaction like this over a mere touch before.

She had never had a reaction like this before. Period.

Slowly, as if her hand were an unarmed grenade and not a part of her own body, Maddison lowered her hand back to her side. Kit was continuing as if nothing had happened, as if he hadn't even felt the pressure of her hand, let alone the almost explosive chemical reaction when skin touched skin.

Which was good, right? No, it was great. No awkwardness, no apologies. She'd just done what any normal person would do at a moment like this. Offered some comfort. Awkward comfort, sure. But all completely appropriate and above board.

'In that moment I was exiled from my home. Came home for holidays and Christmases, pretended I was fine, that there was no problem on my side. But I couldn't stay for long, not while they lived in Kilcanon. It's got worse since he died. I feel it more than ever. Going back gets harder every time. His absence seems larger every time.'

Maddison took a deep breath, steadying her voice as best she could. 'Did she love him?' She badly wanted the answer to be yes. After all, she'd been ready to love Bart, hadn't she? Ready to give him her body and soul in return for the security he guaranteed. She wasn't one of those gold-digging fakes ready to barter themselves away for a lifestyle. She was just cautious, that was all. Not ready to commit her heart too soon. Not till she knew it was safe.

'I'd like to think so, I really do. At least, I hope he believed she did. I hope he died thinking she adored him just as he adored her. Of course, her forthcoming nuptials to an older, richer and more influential man might point the other way but, hey, what do I know about grief?'

'A fair bit from the sound of it,' she said softly and he grimaced.

'It's been three years. It's time I moved on and accepted my responsibilities to the family. That's what my parents think. Not that *they've* really moved on. I'm not sure they'll ever accept the fact that Euan has gone and I am all that's left. Poor seconds.'

'I'm sure they don't think that.'

He laughed, a short bitter sound. 'You've spoken to my mother. You must have worked out what a disappointment I am.'

'I know she wants to hear from you, that messages through me aren't enough.' What would it be like to have a mother who cared? Who tried and tried to get through to you even when you were too grief-stricken and hurt to respond. 'Wait, Eleanor's wedding. Is that the wedding I keep getting calls about?'

'The very same. She's marrying a neighbour of ours and my parents are very insistent that we all go along and bless her new marriage. It's the right thing to do. And they're right, and yet I just can't bring myself to accept the damn invite. It's like if I do, that's it. Euan has gone and it was all for nothing.'

CHAPTER FIVE

IT HAD BEEN a long day and by the time Maddison had noted down the maker of the clock situated just outside the Royal Observatory in Greenwich Park she was beat. She flopped onto a bench with an exaggerated sigh. 'That's half of London off my sightseeing list.'

'See, virtue is its own reward.' Kit had his trademark amused smile back in place as if the heartfelt conversation in Holland Park had never taken place. Maddison couldn't help thinking that it was for the best. She'd mentioned her hopes for Bart, he'd opened up about his brother. They were even. No more depth required. And next weekend she would be armed with an entire list of small talk and safe topics to make sure they went no further.

'Actually...' she smiled sweetly at him '...reward is its own reward. Event of my choosing, remember?' Even as she said the words she wondered if she was playing with fire, spending more time alone with Kit Buchanan. But an event was different; if she chose wisely they wouldn't have to communicate at all. And it all made good copy for her social-media sites. She had a ton of pictures to add over the week: the Japanese garden at Holland Park, another gorgeous garden in the equally gorgeous Chelsea and the slightly disappointing visit to Vauxhall. It was a perfectly adequate park but she had secretly been hoping that the old pleasure gardens were still intact with winding, tree-lined paths full of lurking rakes, and a ballroom brimming with waltzing, masked partygoers. Now that would have got a lot of 'likes'. A few pictures of her dallying with breeches-clad rakes and surely Bart would have been over on the next plane.

Although given the choice she'd have been tempted to stick with the rakes... Maddison pushed the disloyal thought aside. Her plans with Bart were—had been—about forever. She wouldn't throw that away for a rake, no matter how tight his breeches.

Nor for a pair of blue eyes and an easy smile. Not that the owner was offering.

'Of course. Your prize. What's tempting you? Dinner at Nobu, drinks at the Garrick, Shakespeare at The Globe?' Kit leaned against the railings and looked out at the view and, despite herself, Maddison couldn't stop her gaze skimming over his denim-clad rear. The worn jeans fitted him just right; even breeches couldn't improve that posterior. 'Or some sort of concert? Your wish is my command.'

'Seriously, anything?'

'That was the deal. Why?' He turned, his eyes creased, a wicked gleam warning her that she wasn't going to be impressed with his next suggestion. She folded her arms and glared at him. It had as much effect as bombarding him with kittens. 'Do you fancy something more risqué? I'm unshockable, you know, quite happy to take you to a burlesque club or into Soho for something a little edgier if that's what you fancy.'

Maddison had an irrepressible urge to play along, just to see how far he'd go. 'Burlesque is very two years ago. Once you've spent a year learning how to unfold yourself from a giant martini glass in little more than a feather boa it quite takes the mystique away. It was great exercise, though, really worked the abs and the glutes—especially hanging upside down on a rope.'

'I'd pay good money to see that,' he said softly and Maddison barely repressed a shiver as the gleam in his eye intensified, darkened. Maybe she didn't want to find out how far he would go. Maybe she was the one who was happy staying right here.

'I'm out of practice.'

'Isn't that a shame?'

Okay, it was definitely time to change the subject. 'Opera. I'd really like to go to the opera, in Covent Garden.'

The gleam was wiped away as if it had never been. 'Opera?'

'You did say anything,' Maddison pointed out sweetly, enjoying the look of horror on his face.

'True. I am a man of my word. But are you sure? Huge ladies in nighties collapsing and dying over twenty minutes of yowling? Because I'm sure there's a complete extended *Lord of the Rings* trilogy showing somewhere. You, me, twelve hours of orcs?'

'You have a very outdated view of opera. Not

the twenty-minute-dying thing,' she added truthfully. 'That's pretty standard, but the casting and staging is equal to the singing now. But if you really hate the idea I'll go by myself.'

'No, no, I promised. Any preference?'

The temptation to demand a full repertoire of Wagner almost overwhelmed her but she resisted. 'You choose, whatever's on. The experience will be enough.'

He shook his head. 'Opera,' he muttered. 'Okay, caterwauling and extensive death scenes it is, but you have one more task before you fully earn it. I want to walk under the Thames, see if it's worth including in a tour, and as we're so close you can come with me. Tell me if it should be on every tourist's wish list.'

'Walk under the Thames?' Maddison stared up at him. 'I hate to break it to you but I left my scuba-diving stuff at home.'

'Luckily for you there's a staircase and a fully tiled tunnel. No masks or tanks required. I believe it's perfectly safe. About one hundred and twenty years old though so there may be a few cracks...'

Maddison's pulse had already sped up at the

words *walk* and *under* but *cracks* sent it hammering into overdrive. 'Why walk when there are perfectly good bridges and cable cars?'

'History. It was put in to help dock workers get to work on time from the other side of the river. I'm joking, Maddison, it's perfectly safe, not a crack to be seen. The damage from World War II was repaired, well around then I think. It's a great addition to the history tour but I just want to see how long it takes and look for things I can use for a clue. If you really hate the idea then...'

'No. It's fine.' It wasn't but no way was she playing the weak, pathetic female. 'I just think you exceeded the walking quota for today and now here you are adding a whole river's worth of extra steps. I'm just calculating how much it's worth. Interval drinks at the opera for a start.'

It wasn't that she was claustrophobic, not at all. She was fine in her tiny studio, wasn't she? And sure, she didn't like flying, but nobody really liked being cheek by jowl with a bunch of strangers in a tin can in the sky. It was just she didn't like feeling that she had no escape. It was too much like the tiny, airless room in the trailer, the door shut and not being allowed to come out, not even to use the toilet or to get a drink. It was being helpless that got to her. And walking under a river seemed a pretty darn vulnerable thing to do.

'Drinks as well? That might make the actual opera part a little more palatable.' He extended a hand. 'Come along, Miss Carter, we can't be lounging around here all day. We have waters to conquer.'

Why had she agreed when it was obvious how much she didn't want to go into the tunnel? Daniel had probably been much more eager to go into the lions' den—but, unlike Daniel, Maddison had no need to martyr herself. Kit had suggested more than once that she could wait for him by the domed entrance but she brushed his suggestion aside with a curt, 'I'm fine, honestly.'

Which was the least honest thing he had heard this week. Fine didn't usually mean pale, big-eyed and mute.

The entrance to the tunnel was by the Cutty Sark, the permanently moored Victorian clipper, and Kit made a note to try and work the boat into the history quiz—with the Royal Observatory so close it would give treasure hunters a good reason to come this far east. But he didn't stop as he steered Maddison past the tourists queuing up for a tour; if she was going to insist on doing something that so obviously freaked her out, then they should get it over with as soon as possible.

They bypassed the glass door lifts at the tunnel entrance, choosing to access the tunnel through the spiral staircase instead, and began the descent still in silence. There must have been one hundred or so steps and Kit breathed a sigh of relief when they reached the bottom, Maddison still safely by his side.

'Okay, keep your eyes out for clues,' he said as cheerfully as he could, as if a mute, white-faced Maddison were a completely normal companion. 'Interpretation, some carving or plaque we could use. I was wondering about the number of steps but lost count halfway down.'

'So did I.'

'She speaks! So, what do you think?'

Maddison swivelled, taking in the tunnel. It

was, Kit had to admit, less than spectacular, the floor a grubby gravel path, the circular walls curving low overhead, completely covered with white rectangular tiles. A line of lights ran ahead, murkily lighting the way. If he was planning to write a crime novel, then this would make a perfect location. If it weren't for the CCTV and other pedestrians, that was. He stepped aside as a family came by, the children yelling excitedly as their voices echoed off the walls.

'It's a little like being in the Tube. If I didn't know I wouldn't have guessed we were under the river.'

'Those Victorians missed a trick. They should have put in glass walls so we could gaze in delight on the murky depths of the Thames, looking out for shopping trolleys and the occasional body.'

'Charming. I so wish they had.'

'Ready? I'm going to warn you now that we're not getting out the other end; there's not a huge amount to see there and I want to take a closer look at the Cutty Sark.'

'There and back again? That's going to cost ices *and* drinks at the opera.' But her voice wasn't so stilted and her posture more natural. Whatever Maddison had been afraid of obviously hadn't materialized—and she was right: it was very much like walking through a connection tunnel at a Tube station. A long connection tunnel. One the width of the Thames, in fact.

And the Thames was wider than he'd realized. 'Seen anything?' They had walked maybe around five hundred yards and he had yet to see a single identifying item that would make the tunnel suitable as a treasure-hunt destination.

'Not a thing. Maybe there will be something at the other end we can direct them to.' She sounded completely normal now, if a little weary.

The lights flickered and she froze, her eyes wide. Not so normal after all, just putting on a good front. Maybe they would have to exit at the far end after all. Kit wasn't sure he wanted to bring her back through the tunnel if she was going to be so jumpy.

'Maybe, otherwise...' But before he could finish his suggestion the lights flickered again and then a third time, before with no further ceremony simply blinking out. Kit blinked and blinked again, the darkness so very complete he didn't know where the tips of his fingers were, which way he was facing.

'What the…?' he swore softly. 'Maddison, where are you? Are you okay?' She didn't reply but he could hear her breathing, fast, shallow, panicked breaths getting hoarser and hoarser as her breathing sped up.

'Maddison.' He put out a hand, feeling for her, conscious of a mild panic, a little like playing blind man's bluff, that moment when you reach out into the unknown, patting the air gingerly, hoping to touch hair or a sleeve. But there were no answering giggles, just increasingly hoarse breaths. He felt again but his hands brushed nothing more substantial than air. Damn.

'Maddison, it's okay. I'm going to get my phone. It has a light on it. Okay? Just slow down, lass.' The affectionate word slipped from his tongue before he was aware. A word that belonged at home, to a past life, a past time. 'Breathe. Breathe.' He kept speaking in a low, measured voice while he fumbled for his phone, breathing a sigh of relief when he located it. It took him three expletive-ridden tries to press his fingerprint onto the lock screen but eventually the phone was on and he could press the torch icon. Immediately a beam of light sprung out from the back, casting a pale glow over the wall in front of him. He moved it to the side and finally located Maddison.

She was utterly rigid, her eyes wide in shock, the blood completely drained from her face as if she were looking into Hades. Kit reached out and took a hand, wincing at the iciness of her flesh. All thoughts of boundaries and assistants and company policies when it came to line managers and their staff disappeared as he shrugged off his jacket, wrapping it around her and pulling her in tight so that he could rub her arms, her back, her hands, trying desperately to transfer some warmth from him to her. She was shaking now, her teeth chattering, but her breathing slowed as he held her. She still didn't utter a single word.

It could only have been a minute at the most but it felt like an eternity. The silence as absolute as the dark, punctuated only by her panicked breath and his murmured comfort. It was almost a shock when the lights came on with no ceremony, just with a dull flicker. Maddison started, stared at the light—and then burst into tears. Convulsive, silent sobs that racked her body as if they would tear her apart.

'Hey, hey, it's okay.' Kit continued to rub her back, his hands moving in slow, comforting circles, but now the lights were back on, now she was responding to his comfort, albeit in a damp, sobbing way. It was hard for him not to notice just how perfectly his hand fit the contours of her back. How her hair was lightly fragranced, a subtle floral scent that made him think of spring. Of how perfectly she fitted into him, her head under his chin and her breasts—oh, dear God, her breasts—nestled enticingly against his chest.

No, not enticingly. She was in pain and shock. What kind of monster found that enticing?

Her waist was supple and her legs gloriously long. The kind of legs a man wanted wrapped round him…

Kit swallowed, his hands stilling as he tried to push the unwanted, forbidden thoughts away. She was in love with someone else, remember? She wanted a porch swing with that someone, which wasn't a sign of commitment he was fa-

miliar with, it must be some American thing, but
it sounded serious. And even if she weren't...

She was bright and quick and ridiculously attractive, not to mention the perfect breasts and
the long legs and the hair. Girls like Maddison
deserved to be put up on pedestals and wor-
shipped. Even if she were free she wasn't for
him. He didn't deserve her, would never deserve
a woman like her. He deserved shallow and su-
perficial and downright annoying at best. Really
he would be better off on his own. He deserved
a lifetime of loneliness.

After a few minutes during which Kit studiously counted the tiles over her shoulders, anything to take his mind off just how closely they
were pressed together, Maddison's breathing
slowed down to the odd gulp, her sobs trans-
muted to small shudders, her tears finally
stemmed. 'I'm so sorry.' She stepped back and he
was instantly cold, instantly empty. He wanted
to drag her back against him, allow his hands
to explore every inch of her body in a way that
had nothing to do with comfort, everything to
do with lust. Kit's eyes dropped to the lush tilt
of her mouth, swollen from tears, and wanted

to crush it under his until her sobs were a distant memory.

He took a step back of his own. 'That's okay. Come on, let's get out of here.'

'I…I…I'm not good in the dark.'

'You don't have to explain anything.' His voice was gruff as he forced the words out. 'Are you okay to walk? I think we both need a stiff drink.'

Maddison cradled the brandy Kit had insisted on buying for her. 'I am really…'

'Sorry,' he supplied. 'I know. But you don't need to be. There is absolutely nothing to apologize for.'

'A twenty-six-year-old woman so afraid of the dark she has a meltdown? That's beyond an apology.' She buried her head in her hands. 'I am completely pathetic. Do you know I sleep with a night light? Like a little kid?'

She had slept with a night light since she was eight, since the night she had woken to hear a noise snuffling outside her trailer. There were coyotes on the Cape but her mind had immediately jumped to bears—or something worse. Maddison had blinked against the total darkness, heart hammering, mind buzzing with a fear completely alien to her eight-year-old mind.

'Mommy.' But her voice was hoarse with fear, the word barely more than a whisper. 'Mommy?'

At some level she'd known, known even if she could call out it would be no use, that her mother had gone out once she was asleep, that she often went out when Maddison was asleep, known that she was all alone in an old trailer in the middle of the woods. That anyone or anything could come and break into the trailer and nobody was there to save her.

Maddison looked up at Kit, her hands gripping the brandy, and took in a deep, shuddering breath, trying to get the panic back under control, where it belonged. 'You know what I love about living in New York? It's never dark. The light shines in through my window all night long.'

Kit reached over and laid his hand over hers, a warm, comforting clasp. She wanted to lace her fingers through his and hold on tight, let him anchor her to the daylight and the sunshine and the busy city street, pull her out of the darkness of the past.

But only she could do that. She needed security, she needed a family of her own to make up for her long, lonely childhood. She wanted the kind of money that meant walls were always thick, lights were always on and that she never, ever had to spend a night on her own.

'We all have our Achilles' heel,' he said, his fingers a comfortable caress on hers. 'No one has to be strong all the time, Maddison.'

She shook her head. He really didn't get it. 'I do,' she told him as she eased her hand out from under his, ignoring the chill on her now-empty hand in the space where he had touched her, the need for his warmth. 'I do. Weakness makes you vulnerable. Strength, security, that's what counts, Kit.'

He was looking at her as if he wanted to see into the heart of her but her barriers were well crafted and she wasn't letting him in. 'What happened, Maddison?'

She picked up the brandy and took a hefty swig, coughing a little as the strong liquor hit the back of her throat. 'Nothing happened, Kit.

It's just life is like this treasure hunt of yours. There are winners and there are losers and you should know by now, I really like to win.'

CHAPTER SIX

'IS THIS WHAT you were hoping for? Because we can always duck out and do something else. Something that doesn't take quite so long.' Kit stared down at the programme, dismay written all over his face. 'Three acts? *Three.*'

'It's less than three hours in total,' Maddison looked around at the glittering sea of people and suppressed an excited shiver. 'And it could be a lot worse. Just think, it could have been Wagner.'

Kit shuddered dramatically. 'I'm definitely not putting this in the guidebook.'

His voice was a little loud and several heads turned disapprovingly. She elbowed him meaningfully. 'It's culture, you have to include it. You can't assume everyone is going to be a philistine just because you are. Besides, you must have known what to expect. This can't be your first opera.'

'Oh, it can. It will also be my last,' he said

darkly. 'I didn't realize your cooperation would have quite so high a price. And I'm not just talking about the tickets—or these gin and tonics.'

Maddison repressed a smile. He might be acting all grumpy, but Kit had gone well above and beyond their agreement. 'Thank you.' She squeezed his arm. 'I didn't expect a gala night. This is really incredible.' She managed to stop the next words tumbling out before her sophisticated girl-about-town image was well and truly blown, but she couldn't keep her eyes from shining her gratitude. *No one has ever done anything like this for me before...*

Maddison looked around for the umpteenth time, trying to keep her excitement locked down deep inside. *Play it cool, Maddison Carter, you belong here.* And tonight she really did. Kit hadn't just brought her to the Royal Opera House, he'd gone all out and hired a box at a first-night gala performance of *Madame Butterfly.*

The cause was fashionable, the tickets sought after and London's great and good were out in force, the women's jewels competing with the huge, dazzling chandeliers, the men in exquisitely cut tuxedos. It was like stepping back in time to Edwardian England—and she, Maddison Carter, was right in the middle of it. A real Buccaneer. She might not own any heirloom jewels, but the man on her arm was one of the most striking in the room and she had intercepted more than one envious glance in their direction.

And everything was fine. She'd been worried on Monday that he would be careful with her, that her breakdown would change his attitude. It had been a relief when he had been his usual, slightly annoying self. In fact it was as if the weekend, the confidences, had never happened. Which was as it should be, because there had been moments when she had felt far too close to him, far too at ease.

Far too attracted.

Maddison sipped her drink, the sharp notes of the gin and tonic a relief. Where had that thought come from? Tunnels aside, she was having a good time with her extracurricular work, but treasure hunts and a heart to heart weren't going to get her the happy-ever-after, all-American dream, were they? She needed to remember her goals: a good marriage, a family of her own, security—emotionally and financially.

She took another sip. Tomorrow. She'd remember it tomorrow. It would be rude not to give her total concentration to the night ahead.

'Do you actually like opera?' Kit murmured in her ear, his breath warm, intimate, on her bare shoulder.

She turned to face him, pushing the disquieting thoughts away. 'I love it.' He arched a disbelieving eyebrow and she laughed. 'Honestly. I grew up with it. How could I not?'

For the first time, discomfort twisted in her as she stretched the truth. She *had* grown up with opera, but not in the way she was implying.

Every summer, Maddison would pick out the men she hoped were her long-lost father and watch them, waiting for recognition to spark in their eyes. Only it never did. They didn't even notice her. The year she turned ten she'd spent the summer hanging out on the beach all day, pretending as usual that she belonged to one of the laughing, happy families enjoying their vacation by the sea. Pretend that any moment they would look up, see her and call her, pull her sand-covered body in close, wrap her in a towel, hand her an ice-cold drink while alternating between kisses and scolding her for straying so far away.

It was so much better than the reality—an empty trailer and cold leftovers. If she was lucky.

Her favourite families owned or rented houses right on the beach. As evening fell and the beach emptied she would sit in the dunes and watch them. And that was when she had first noticed him, the tall, broad man who lifted his daughter up with one hand, who spent hours constructing the perfect sandcastle, who sang opera as he grilled dinner for his family on the beachhouse patio.

She watched him every summer until the year she turned fourteen and realized that daydreams were never going to change anything.

But she couldn't shed the knowledge that if she'd lived with him, with somebody like him, with her real father, then maybe she would have had the childhood she wanted, the one she invented for herself as soon as she left Bayside: a childhood filled with singing arias, with ballet matinees and Saturday trips to the museum. The moment she hit New York she tried to re-create that childhood and fill in the gaps in her knowledge, spending her wages on cheap matinee seats up in the gods, museum tours, absorbing a childhood's worth of culture.

And it had brought her here, to the most glamorous place she had ever been in her entire life.

Her little black-and-white dress might be on the demure side but it held its own, every perfect seam screaming its quality. She smoothed out the heavy material with a quiet prayer of gratitude to the woman who had hired Maddison as a maid, giving her a room when Maddison left home at sixteen. Thanks to Mrs Stanmeyer, Maddison had had the space and time to study her last two years at school—and her benefactress's influence had secured Maddison a scholarship and bursary at a private liberal arts college in New Hampshire. In its ivy-covered buildings she'd both got her degree and reinvented herself.

And she never forgot Mrs Stanmeyer's advice: Maddison only bought the very best of everything. It meant her wardrobe was limited but it was timelessly classy and made to last. It allowed her to fit in anywhere.

The past faded away as the music swelled and surrounded her. Every note exquisite, every aria a dream. She squeezed her eyes shut and let the music take over, offering wordless thanks to the man in the beach house. He wasn't Maddison's real father, she knew that now—truthfully she'd known it then—but he'd given her a gift nonetheless. She might have had to train herself to appreciate this music, but her training wheels were long since discarded and she was all-in. Every atom of her.

Finally the last lingering note died away and the audience was frozen in that delicious moment between performance and applause. Still tingling, Maddison turned to Kit. Had he hated it? Was he bored? She really hoped he got it.

That he understood a part of her.

His eyes were open and alert, which was a definite bonus; Bart liked to see and be seen doing culturally highbrow activities, but Maddison suspected if he could have got away with earplugs he would have—as it was she wasn't convinced he didn't snooze the best part of any performance away. Kit, however, was leaning forward, his arm on the balustrade and his eyes fixed onto the stage below.

She couldn't wait any longer. 'So? Did you hate it? You hated it. If you're bored we should go. Honestly...'

Kit reached out and covered her gesturing hand with his, sparks igniting up and down her arm as his fingers clasped hers. 'I wasn't bored. I...I don't know if I'm enjoying it exactly. I mean, offer me a trade for a sticky, beer-covered floor, some drums and guitars and a mosh pit and I'd take it, but I have to admit I'm...' he paused, raking a hand through his hair '...moved.'

'That's a start.' The glow inside was gladness. She'd introduced him to something new, something life enhancing. It had nothing to do with the hand still holding hers, nothing at all. 'Would you come again?'

There was no pause this time. 'Yes. Yes, I would.' Surprise lit up his face as he spoke. 'Wow, that was unexpected. I didn't know I was going to say that.' His fingers tightened, a cool clasp blazing a heated trail straight up her arm. 'Thank you.'

Maddison tried not to look at their entwined

hands, not to behave as if this was in any way odd. 'For what?'

'For making me try something new.' The words were simply said but his gaze held a barely concealed smoulder, one that ignited every nerve right down to her bare toes.

'You're very welcome.' She tried to sound non-committal but couldn't stop the soft smile curving her lips, couldn't stop her eyelashes fluttering down in an unexpectedly shy gesture. What was going on? This wasn't how she operated. She hadn't tried to learn him by heart, hadn't tried to mould herself into what she thought he wanted. She was being herself, as much as she ever could be, thinking of nothing but work and yet unexpectedly finding herself having fun.

It had been a long time since fun had figured in her plans.

By some unspoken mutual accord their hands unclasped as Kit ushered her from the box to collect their interval drinks.

The corridors were buzzing with people, the bar even more so. Luckily there was no queuing; instead, here in the rarefied environs of the dress circle on a gala night, trays of champagne and canapés were circling amongst the chattering crowds. Kit neatly snagged two glasses off a passing waitress and passed one to Maddison, raising his own glass to her as he did so.

'To trying new things.' His eyes gleamed a bright blue in the glittering lights, a devilish glint flickering in the depths. Maddison's mind whirled with confusion, with an unexpected, unwanted desire to press a little closer. For those eyes to look at her with even more heat, more devilry. Her dizziness increased as his eyes held hers, the rest of the room falling away.

This was it, a dim, distant part of her analysed as she stood there, staring up at him. This was what attracted Camilla and her ilk to him, even though he warned them away, warned them that he wasn't in it for the medium-term, let alone forever. But when he focused, really focused, he could make a girl feel as if she were the only person worth knowing in the room. The only person *in* the room.

And yet she was pretty sure he didn't do it on purpose; this was no practised trick, no calculated seductive move.

That was what made it so dangerous, made him so very dangerous.

Even she, mistress of her own heart and destiny, might get swept away. For a very little while.

Or not… She was too seasoned a player to fold her hand at the first eye contact and warm, intimate glance. Maddison took a deep breath, stepping back, out of the seductive circle of his spell. 'To new things,' she agreed. 'It's the ballet next.'

Kit smiled appreciatively. 'Oh, no, it's my turn to choose next and I quite fancy seeing the demure and always put-together Maddison Carter in a mosh pit. Up for it?'

A what? Maddison opened her mouth to deliver what was definitely going to be a stinging retort as soon as she could think of one, when a languid hand draped itself on Kit's shoulder, a statuesque middle-aged brunette spinning him around as she pressed a kiss onto his suddenly rigid cheek. Only a muscle beating in his jawline showed any emotion.

Maddison shivered, suddenly chilled. Had they turned the air conditioning up? Hard to imagine how very warm she'd been just a few seconds before.

'Kit, dearest. I thought it was you but Charles said I must be mistaken. Kit at the opera! And yet here you are...'

Kit was still supremely still, only that pulsing muscle and the flash of anger in his eyes betraying any sign of life. 'Not mistaken, Laura. Hello, Charles.' He nodded over Laura's shoulder at the tall, balding man behind her.

'Gracious, Kit, last place I would have expected to see you. Not your usual style of thing.'

'No,' he agreed, his voice smooth. 'It's not. It is, however, very much Maddison's style and so here you find me.' He smoothly stepped out of Laura's possessive clasp and took Maddison's arm, ushering her forward, his hand holding her tight as if he feared she might run—or that he might. 'Laura, Charles, this is Maddison Carter. Maddison, this is Charles and Laura Forsyth.' He paused then before continuing, his voice still as urbanely smooth as the richest cream. 'Eleanor's parents.'

'Lovely to meet you.' Her words were as mechanical as her smile, Maddison's mind sprinting ahead as she watched Laura Forsyth's unsubtle summing up. Maddison held her chin up, as unconcerned as if she hadn't noticed the slow appraisal; she had nothing to hide, clothes-wise at least. Her outfit might be demure but the quality was unmistakable.

'American? How long are you over for? So nice of Kit to take you around.'

Maddison's eyes narrowed at the thinly hidden derisive note in the older woman's voice. Did Laura Forsyth think she could be put down so easily? It had been a long time since Maddison had allowed herself to be dismissed in a couple of sentences.

She would wipe that smile right off Mrs Forsyth's suspiciously wrinkle-free face.

Maddison plastered a bright smile on to her own naturally wrinkle-free thank you very much face and moved even closer to Kit, slipping under his arm, her own snaking round his waist as she turned to him. 'Isn't it? Kit's being very hospitable.' Maddison laid an extra-slow drawl onto the last two words, filling them with an unmistakable innuendo, and felt him quiver but whether it was with humour or anger she had no idea.

What the heck was she doing? Had she taken leave of her senses? She picked *now* to lose her temper, to behave spontaneously? It was going to look great on her résumé when Kit fired her. Reason for dismissal? Inappropriate temptress at the opera.

The older woman's eyes narrowed. 'He always was good-hearted, weren't you, Kit? Eleanor always said you put yourself out for others. We will be seeing you next week, won't we? It would mean a lot to Eleanor. After all, you're still family. I *had* hoped that, well, never mind that now. But for Euan's sake, Kit, you should come to her wedding.' Her eyes flickered towards Maddison. 'You are welcome to bring a guest, of course.'

'That's very kind of you, Laura. I am very busy and we weren't sure we could spare the time, were we, Maddison? But it would be a shame not to show you Scotland while you're here. So, thank you, Laura. We'd love to accept. Please do pass my apologies on to Eleanor for taking so long to respond.'

We? Hang on a second. Maddison worked to

keep her smile in place. He was calling Laura Forsyth's bluff, surely. He didn't actually expect Maddison to attend a wedding in Scotland. With him. With his whole family. His ex-girlfriend and dead brother's widow's wedding. Did he?

There weren't enough opera tickets in the world.

The smile faltered on Laura Forsyth's face. 'How lovely. Eleanor will be delighted. We'd better get on. Charles has clients here. I'll see you—both—next weekend.' She kissed Kit again before disappearing into the crowd.

Maddison freed herself and rounded on Kit. He looked completely unruffled.

She folded her arms and glared at him. 'What did you just do?'

'Accepted the wedding invitation.' How could he look so calm and so darn amused? Did he think this was funny? 'After all, you've been reminding me to for weeks. I thought you'd be pleased.'

Thought she'd be *what*? 'I don't care whether you go or not, I just wanted you to decide either way and for the many, many phone calls to stop. I wanted you to make a decision for you. Not for me! Why did you do that? Now she'll think that I… That we…'

'She thought that the second you cosied into me. It wouldn't have been gentlemanly of me to push you away and explain that, sorry, you were my over-familiar assistant, and once she had included you in the invitation it seemed rude to accept for just me.'

Okay, she *had* been the one pressing in close in a proprietary fashion. 'I shouldn't have…' how had he put it? '…cosied into you like that. It was silly. It was just the way she looked at me. I got mad.' This was why she kept her temper, her feelings, under close control—usually, at least. Look what trouble acting impulsively could do.

'Apology accepted.' Maddison nearly choked at his smooth words. 'And now you've accepted responsibility for the whole situation you can see it's too late to backtrack now.' His mouth curved wickedly and she didn't know whether she wanted to wipe the smile off his face—or kiss it off.

Wipe, definitely wipe.

'Too late? I could have had plans. I might have plans.' Kit shot her a knowing look and Maddison scowled. 'Okay, I don't have plans but she doesn't know that. Just tell her I mixed up my dates. Or I'm ill. Or I had to leave the country.'

'Or you could just come with me.'

Maddison stilled. 'Why?'

Kit shrugged. 'Why not? Scotland is beautiful, especially at this time of year, and you really should see more of the UK than just London.'

'Your family will be there.'

'That's okay, they don't bite. You'll be doing me a favour, actually. I think I mentioned that I don't go back often. It can be a little intense. Your presence will relax things a little.'

'You want me to come along to act as a buffer between you and your parents?'

'I said no such thing. You speak to my mother more than I do. She'll be delighted to meet you at last.'

Meet the parents. Not at all awkward. 'Isn't there someone else you'd rather take? An actual real date?'

Kit stilled. 'I don't introduce my dates to my parents.'

'Not ever?' Obviously she never had but there were mitigating circumstances in her case. Kit's

mother sounded both sober and present, quali-
ties Maddison's mother had failed to possess.

'Not since Euan died. No, not because I'm too
heartbroken.' Her face must have expressed her
thoughts and Maddison flushed with embarrass-
ment. 'No. Introducing dates to parents raises
hopes in bosoms on both sides and that's something I'd rather not do.'

His words on her birthday came back to her.
'You really don't want to fall in love again one
day?'

'No.' His voice was uncompromising. 'I don't
believe in love. It's just getting carried away by
infatuation and circumstance.'

His views weren't so far away from Maddison's own but it was uncomfortable hearing
them so baldly stated.

'Look, Maddison, it's a good opportunity for
you to spend some time outside London. Besides, we can work on the way up. I'm quite
happy to dictate and drive.'

'You're really selling it to me. A weekend of
weddings and work.'

'If you really hate the idea, then of course you

don't have to come. But I do know it will be much more fun if you're there.'

Fun? With her? Warmth stole through her at the casual words. Words of acceptance and liking. 'Okay.' Wow, she was easily bought, wasn't she? But Kit was right. She should get out of London and see more while she was here. It had taken her twenty-six years to get to Europe; what if it was another twenty-six before she returned?

And he thought she was fun…not competent or organized or reliable. Fun.

'Great. I hope you brought some warm clothes. Scotland can be nippy even in early summer and I get the impression the atmosphere at Eleanor's wedding will be positively frosty.'

CHAPTER SEVEN

'ARE WE THERE YET?' Kit looked over as Maddison stretched and yawned, noting that she looked more catlike than ever as she did so. Her hair was a little mussed up from sleeping in the car, her face make-up free. She looked younger, freer. His stomach tightened. If only they were on their way to somewhere where *he* could feel free. Instead every mile closer to the border the air closed in just a little bit more. Duty, responsibility, expectation all waiting to descend on him like an unwanted coronation mantle.

He turned the radio down a little. 'Not even close, I'm afraid. It would help if this section of the motorway wasn't all roadworks—it feels like we're permanently stuck at fifty miles per hour.' It might have made more sense to fly or to get the train but Kit needed to know that he had an escape plan ready and active at all times—and that meant his own transport.

'I don't understand. We've been on the road for hours. England just can't be that big. It's meant to be all little and quaint.' Maddison stared out of the window at the never-ending fields—and the never-ending drizzle—as if she were searching for thatched roofs and maypoles. She'd be searching for some time. The view from the M6 was many things but quaint wasn't one of them.

Besides, there was something she needed to be put right on. '*England* is nearly four hundred miles long and we're driving about three quarters of the length of it, but, as you need to remember before you are thrown out of the country for disrespect, we're not going to be in England, we're going to Scotland. A whole different country.' Despite himself, despite everything, Kit could hear the pride in his voice, feel the slight swell in his chest. Eleanor used to tease him that the further north they got the broader his accent got. Of course, now she rolled her *r*'s as if her home counties upbringing and Oxbridge education belonged to someone else, more Scottish than Edinburgh rock.

'A whole different country,' Maddison repeated. 'Like Canada?'

'But without border patrols and with the same currency.'

'Got it.' She slid him a sidelong glance. 'Are you okay?'

'Fine, why?'

'It can't be easy, watching your ex get married.'

If only she knew the half of it. 'I've had plenty of practice. This is her second wedding and she's still in her twenties. I fully expect to watch Eleanor get married several more times before she's through.'

'It's just...' she hesitated '...Eleanor's mother seemed concerned, as if she thinks you're still in love with the bride.'

'She hopes I'm still in love with the bride,' Kit said drily. 'I bet right now she's instructing the vicar to leave a good long pause after the true impediment part so that I can stand up and claim Eleanor for my own.'

'Leaving me weeping in the aisles?' There was an appreciative gurgle in Maddison's voice as she outlined the scenario. 'If only I had a hat, one with a little veil. Oh! And gloves.'

'There's no need to sound like you want it to happen.'

'I'm just saying if it were to happen I'd want to be appropriately dressed. What's the groom like?'

'Loaded, huge estate in Argyll, another one much further up in the Highlands—rich folk pay a fortune for the hunting and fishing. Plus various concerns in the city, a town house in Edinburgh. He's a catch...'

'I can tell there's an *if* or a *but* coming up.'

To hell with it, he needed to be honest with someone. '*If* you like your life partner to be the other side of forty-five, red-faced, balding and a pontificating know-it-all.'

'He sounds gorgeous.' She hesitated. 'So why?'

'Hmm?'

'I kind of got the impression that Eleanor's parents were all about the money and the image. Aren't they glad she's marrying someone who can keep her in style? An estate sounds pretty grand.'

'The Forsyths all about the money? Whatever gave you that idea?'

'So don't take this the wrong way, you're a nice

guy when you want to be and easy enough on the eye, but why does socially ambitious mama want her darling daughter to run off with you? Especially as she already jilted you once?'

'She didn't jilt me. We were never engaged.' Thank goodness.

'You know what I mean. It doesn't make any sense. Unless she's thinking about her grandkids and the gene pool. No male-pattern baldness in your family.' She looked at his hair as if assessing the thickness.

Kit suppressed a sigh; this persistence was useful in his assistant, completely necessary if she was road-testing a treasure hunt. It was a little less comfortable when she was probing into his past. His hands gripped the steering wheel tight, his eyes fixed on the grey lines of the motorway as he eased his way past a lorry. 'As the youngest son I *wasn't* much of a catch. I was a student with his own eccentric business. I didn't plan on going into the City or doing any of the respectable money-making jobs a suitable partner for the Forsyths' beautiful only daughter would do.'

'A girl's gotta eat.' There was something oddly constrained in her voice despite the light words.

'She does. The right food at the right tables in the right households.' Kit hesitated. He liked that as far as Maddison was concerned he was her boss, nothing less, nothing more. But she was going to find out exactly what the future held for him in approximately four hours' time anyway and he would rather she heard it from him. Warts, title and all. Kit took a long drink of water, handing the bottle back to Maddison and focusing on the road ahead as he chose his words carefully. 'Euan was the eldest son and that made him a much better prospect than me. The Buchanans aren't as rich, not nearly as rich, as Angus Campbell, the lucky groom. But our name is older, we have a title, an ancient one, not an honorary one, and the castle has been in our family for generations. For new money like the Forsyths, that's worth more than a second estate. Now Euan's gone…'

He could hear Maddison's breath quicken. What was it with the predatory urge that overtook formerly sane women at the mention of a title and a castle? Kit didn't want to turn and look at her, to see if her eyes were gleaming covetously.

She shifted. 'You're no longer the second son. What does that mean?'

'Mean? It means that I'm the heir. To the title, the estate and the family name.' He laughed but there was no humour in the sound, just the bitter twist of fate. 'Turns out Eleanor bet on the wrong brother all those years ago and she's been kicking herself about it ever since we buried Euan.' Kit was trying to sound matter-of-fact but there was a rawness he couldn't cover. It was a long, long time since Eleanor had had the ability to hurt him. It turned out Kit was completely capable of destroying his own life—and the lives of everyone around him—without her help.

But she'd duped Euan and he would never forgive her for that.

'You don't know that,' Maddison argued. 'She might have really fallen in love with your brother. Hard on you, sure, but just because he was the eldest, just because he was going to inherit stuff, it doesn't mean she used you.'

He swallowed, his mouth dry despite the water he'd just consumed. 'Ah, but you see she told me. A month after we buried Euan. A month after she stood weeping by his grave and shooting me sympathetic glances as I had to come to terms with the knowledge that my brother had died...' The guilt that never really left him pressed down, heavier than ever. Such a stupid death. Such an unnecessary death. And he was to blame... 'She came to me and said she'd made a terrible mistake all those years ago. That she had never stopped loving me. That she knew it was too soon but maybe one day...'

Maddison was staring at him open-mouthed. 'She said all that?'

'Of course, I had just sold that quirky little start-up for a few million quid and a nice, well-paid and respectable job. Add the title and the castle to that and suddenly her old lover was looking all shiny and new. She still had her sights on being the Lady of Kilcanon.'

'I'll bet. What did you say?'

'I said not on her life. And then I got very, very drunk.' His hands tightened on the wheel. All those years of bitterness, the loss of his brother, all because of some *princess* who thought she was entitled to have it all—and damn anyone who got in her way.

But in the end he couldn't blame Eleanor for

Euan's death. No. The only person to blame was Kit. And he could never, ever atone. God knew he had tried.

Maddison watched the scenery flash by but if someone quizzed her about what she had seen she would have definitely flunked the test. It was starting to add up: Kit's lack of interest in anything but the most perfunctory of relationships, his reluctance to go back to Scotland. He must have loved Eleanor very much once. Until she betrayed him.

Betrayal was such a strong word. After all, what had Eleanor done, exactly? Married strategically? Could Maddison blame her for that? After all, wasn't that her goal?

But she wasn't prepared to trample over sibling relationships and break hearts to do it. Her case was totally different. Wasn't it?

But the moral high ground didn't feel all that high.

'This must all come as a shock to you.'

She started. 'Sorry? The castle? Yeah, that's unexpected. Is there a moat and dungeons? A talking candlestick? A butler?'

'No to all the above and no, I didn't mean the castle. I meant the unhappily ever after. You believe in love at first sight, don't you?'

She almost laughed. As if. Nothing could be further from the truth; she wasn't even sure she believed in love. Lust, sure, although she tried to ignore it. It could take a girl horribly off track. Affection, definitely. Compatibility. They were the foundations of a good, solid relationship. Shared goals another. But true love? That was for fairy tales. If Maddison had sat in her trailer waiting to be rescued she'd still be sitting there now. 'What makes you say that?'

'Mr Grow Old on a Porch Swing. What happened when you first saw him? Cupid's arrow straight to your heart?'

'Not exactly.' The mocking tone in his voice hit her harder than any arrow could.

'So what was it? What attracted you to him? How did you know he was the one if you weren't instantly smitten?'

Maddison thought back to the party where she and Bart had first met. It had been thrown by one of her college friends who had just bought, with family money, a fabulous loft apartment on the

Upper East Side. Bart had been lounging against one of the carefully distressed brick walls, deep in conversation with a couple of friends. He had just looked so *solid*: tall, broad, blonde, clean-cut with that indefinable privileged air that Maddison worked so hard to cultivate but feared she never could. He wasn't handsome, not exactly, but he was nice to look at—and she could instantly see a future with him. A safe future. She had had no idea who he was at the time—her ambitions were high but not *that* high. But she could tell by his clothes, his stance, his air that he had the background she looked for, the future she needed. He had obviously felt her staring because he had broken off the conversation to look over at her—and then he had smiled and she had been lost in a world of infinite possibilities. A world where she was safe. For a time at least.

'I…' She stopped, unable to go on, and twisted her fingers in her lap, trying to find the right words. But what words were right? She didn't want to lie to him—she who lied to everyone—but there was no truth palatable enough to be served up.

Kit winced. 'I'm sorry, Maddison, it's not been

that long, has it? I'm forgetting that not everyone weeps crocodile tears. For what it's worth, anyone who needs a break from you is an absolute idiot. He's not going to meet anyone better.'

No? He might meet someone genuine, someone who wanted Bart for his conversation and body, for his passions and interests, not for their vision of a perfect future. Could she really have done it? Married someone for convenience? Oh, she hadn't used that word before, had she? But that was what it came down to. She had deceived Bart—and she had deceived herself. 'He should. He deserves to. He's a really nice guy. Maybe he was right to call a halt to things.'

'Oh?' He raised an enquiring eyebrow.

Maddison hadn't told anyone the truth for so long there were times she wasn't sure exactly what the truth *was* any more. Not the teachers at school when they had asked about her mom, not her friends, not herself. Especially not herself. And Kit would judge her, he more than most. Maybe that was what she deserved.

Before she could weigh up the consequences of carrying on she spoke, the words almost tumbling out in the rush to unburden herself at long last. 'Bart's full name is Bartholomew J Van De Grierson III.'

But of course that meant nothing to him. 'Poor guy. I thought Christopher Alexander Campbell Buchanan was bad enough.'

She ignored him. 'His family have lived in New York going back to colonial times. They're as close as we have to aristocracy, or to royalty. Bart works in the family business, and by business I mean global, multimillion, fingers in pies you've never heard of and plenty that you will have. He owns this incredible brownstone and the family have an estate in the Hamptons, right by the sea. It's as big as a small village.'

'Right. You found out all the important things, then?'

She had—and they had terrified her and seduced her in equal measure. She'd been in well over her head but how could she turn her back on the possibility of a future so glittering it obliterated her more modest dreams? She stared at her hands. 'Have you ever been hungry, Kit? Have you ever woken up to find out that the electricity was turned off and there's no hot water for a shower? Have you ever had to work out which clothes were the least dirty and turn up for school in them?'

He shot her a quick look but she wouldn't, couldn't meet his eye. 'I wasn't prom queen and I didn't have a credit card on Daddy's account. I didn't *have* a daddy. And my mom wasn't around much.' She took a deep breath. 'I want a family of my own, Kit. I want security. I want to know that I'm not just a pay cheque away from eviction, that there is always, always money in the bank. I want kids.'

'Four of them. I remember.'

She swallowed. How had he remembered that? 'Four children who will have the safest, happiest, most perfect childhood ever. And I know that people say money doesn't buy happiness— but I bet you anything those people have never gone to bed hungry. Or been really, really cold. So cold they can't sleep and their bones ache.'

'No, they probably haven't. So Bart wanted four kids too? He was happy to be your secure happy ever after?'

She laughed. 'People like Bart don't marry people like me, Kit. You must know that. Money calls to money. Sure, he might date a girl like me, walk on the wrong side of the tracks for a little bit, but he wouldn't bring her home to meet the parents, wouldn't take her away with his friends. Wouldn't marry her. I grew up in a small town by the ocean and I saw it all the time—the wealthy summer visitors only mixed with people like them. And I knew that if I wanted to be one of them then I had to transform.' She couldn't stop now she'd started, the words spilling out. It was cathartic; this must be what confession was like, handing over your sins for someone else to absolve or punish.

'Transform?'

'Into one of them. Normal, a little spoiled, entitled. I got to college and created a whole new identity—a prom-queen, cheerleading, hayride, ice-carnival princess identity. Not too detailed, not too fancy, not privileged enough to raise alarm bells but privileged enough for the right groups to let me in. The college I went to was full of prep-school graduates with the right kind of background. It was almost too easy in the end to infiltrate them. By the time I graduated and moved to New York I knew the right kind of people with the right kind of connections to take me to the Upper East Side and from there…'

'You hooked him.'

'I couldn't believe it,' she half whispered. 'I wanted someone from a solid, wealthy background but Bart was beyond my wildest dreams. I worked really hard to turn myself into the right kind of wife for him—made sure I found out about the things he liked, got on with his friends, stuck to the rules. I wasn't clingy or needy or argumentative or sulky. I dressed the way he liked, wore my hair the way he liked, cooked the right food, hiked or swam or played tennis, whatever he was in the mood for. I read the right books…' She gulped in air, shocked by the bitter tint to her voice. 'But in the end I still wasn't good enough. He walked away anyway. It serves me right for aiming too high.' Brought down like Icarus, her punishment for flying too close to the sun.

Kit didn't answer for a long moment and Maddison couldn't look at him to see his reaction. Disgust, probably, maybe dislike. Hatred. After all, she was everything he abhorred. Fake, money-grabbing, conniving…

'Maybe you didn't know him as well as you thought.'

That wasn't what she'd expected him to say. 'What do you mean?'

'Have you been pretending the last few weeks? With me?'

'No, I mean, you're my boss, not...'

'Not a suitable future husband?'

She nodded, mortified heat flooding her. 'I mean, you have a good job and all, and I didn't know about the castle.' Maddison winced. Honesty was probably not the best policy here; she wasn't helping herself sound any better. 'It wouldn't have made any difference anyway. I want the life I missed out on, you know, the prom-queen and hayride life, summers at the shore and clambakes, Fourth of July parties and huge family Thanksgivings life. It's all I've ever wanted. Much as I could come to love London, that life doesn't exist here.'

'All I'm saying is that maybe Bart fell in love with the girl I've come to know. She's witty and clever and annoyingly organized, if a bit too partial to long operas. Maybe he wanted that Maddison, not the Stepford wife you turned yourself into. Just a thought.'

His words sank in slowly, each one dropping perilously close to her heart. 'I thought you'd hate me.'

Kit's face was completely impassive, a muscle beating in his cheek a lone sign her confession affected him at all. 'We've all done things in the past we need to atone for. I'm the last person to judge anyone. But if I were you I'd stop trying so hard. Just be yourself. Do you really think money will bring you happiness?'

Maddison winced. It sounded so cold put like that. 'I know security will...'

'Then make your own. You're a clever woman with a great career ahead of her. I'd advise you to concentrate on that. Marriage to the wealthiest man in the world can't bring you security, Maddison. Just look at Eleanor. She thought she had it made and it all disappeared, leaving her to start again. Bachelor Number Two may be wealthier but he's a bitterer pill to swallow.'

Make her own security? She'd spent so long focusing on just one possible path it hadn't even occurred to her that there could be more than one way to her goal. Maybe she could buy her own apartment in the city, have her own summer house at the shore. Maybe if she relaxed then she'd meet someone who wanted a family as much as she did, who didn't need luring into commitment.

Maybe there was a happy ever after waiting out there for her after all. She stole a glance at Kit, his face still completely unreadable. One thing she knew for sure was that her future didn't include messy brown hair, blue eyes and a lilting accent. Kit Buchanan's idea of long-term was next-day dinner reservations. And that was fine. The ache in her chest wasn't some inexplicable sense of loss. Not at all. She might be considering moving the goalposts but she hadn't changed as much as that. Had she?

CHAPTER EIGHT

'Is THIS IT? Are we in Kilcanon?' Maddison craned her head. 'I can't see a castle. When you said castle did you mean small cottage because, I have to tell you, they're not the same thing where I come from.'

'No, this is Loch Lomond. I need to stretch my legs. Fancy a walk?'

'A walk?'

'It's when people move at a slow pace putting one foot in front of the other in order to get across ground.'

'I know what a walk is. I just…I mean…I wasn't sure whether you wanted company.'

'I could leave you in the car but that seems a little inhospitable.'

But he knew what she meant. She was trying to sound him out, to see if he still wanted her company after her revelations just a couple of hours earlier. Maddison had lapsed into silence after her sudden and startling confession, leaving Kit to sort through a myriad conflicting thoughts and feelings: sorrow, sympathy, disgust. Admiration.

She hadn't said much about her childhood but he could fill in the bleak gaps; her need to be in control at all times, her fear of the dark, it all made sense. As did her overwhelming desire for security.

Her targeting of a rich man to be that security was a little harder to stomach, a little too close to home, and his first instinct had been to drive her to the airport at Glasgow and send her back to London on the next plane. The last thing he needed to do was take another gold-digger back to meet the family.

But she was no Eleanor and he was a lot older and a lot wiser. At least Maddison was honest about who she was and what she wanted. And could he blame her for trying to re-create the mythologized childhood of her dreams?

No. He didn't blame her or dislike her or even pity her. Truth be told he kind of admired her. Life had thrown every disadvantage at her and she had risen above it, made something of herself. So she had made some mistakes along the way? It was better than hiding away, bitter and resentful, or being too afraid to try.

Like you? He pushed the thought away. He wasn't bitter or afraid, he was undeserving. Undeserving of happiness or of love.

Maddison, on the other hand, deserved a lifetime of both.

She joined him at the path, a light Puffa slung on over her jumper and jeans. 'This is a real loch? Is there a monster in it?'

'Several. Don't walk too close to the edge or they might pull you in, kelpies and boobries and...'

'Stop. You know what I mean. A *real* monster.'

'You need to be a lot further north for Nessie, I'm afraid. But if you're lucky you might see a selkie when we get to Kilcanon—watch the seals closely, they're usually the larger ones.'

'I'll do that.' She hesitated. 'Kit, about earlier?'

'It's fine. I'm glad you told me but you don't owe me any explanation, Maddison. We're colleagues, that's all.' But the words sounded hollow even to his own ears.

'Good. I've never...I mean, I don't talk about

myself very often. Thank you. For listening and not hating me.'

'I could never hate you.' In a different time, if he were a different man, he might be in danger of exactly the opposite. But his heart was frozen somewhere back in time and he had no intention of allowing it to be melted, not even by this fiery American survivor.

It was a bright, warmish day and Maddison was soon far too hot in the thick jacket she had layered over her sweater. 'You told me it would be cold and raining.'

'It could well be when we get to Kilcanon. It's a microclimate. All of Scotland is.'

'Is it as pretty as here?' She stopped and turned, admiring once again the blue waters lapping gently against the loch shore and the hills rising steeply on every side, greens and purples and shadowy greys. She had thought that they would head down to the loch but instead Kit had chosen a path that led away, a steep path winding up into the hills. Turned out even regular running didn't prepare you for hill-climbing. Maddison could already feel a pull on her calves and her lungs were beginning to make themselves felt.

'Pretty? There's nothing pretty about Kilcanon. It's magnificent... Here, watch out. This is a bit slippy.' Kit extended a hand and pulled Maddison up the slick, steep rock. His grip was firm and she had a sudden urge to lean on him, to allow him to guide her up the narrow, slippery path, but she quelled it firmly, brushing past him instead to take the lead.

'Come on, Buchanan,' she called over her shoulder as she set off at a pace, shocked at how her lungs burnt as she pulled herself up. She had really got out of condition recently; this would do her good. Besides, giving her body a good workout might cure it of some treacherous urges—such as wanting to stare into Kit's eyes, keep hold of his hands or lean into that solid strength.

Oh, no, she was getting sappy. Maddison increased her pace, enjoying the ache in her calf muscles, the fiercer pull in her thighs, the heave in her chest. The distance she was putting between him and her.

'It's not a race, Carter. Slow down and smell the roses—or at least enjoy the view.'

'Slowing down is for losers. You'd be eaten alive in Manhattan,' she threw back as she concentrated on one foot in front of the other, using her hands and upper body to pull her up a particularly vertiginous twist in the path. All she was aware of was the steep rise of the way ahead, the rocks that needed to be navigated, the small treacherous pebbles that could cause a foot to slip, the slicks of mud and the...

'No! Darn it!'

And the deceptively deep puddles. This one calf deep and full of thick mud, cold as it sucked at her foot and leg.

'Ugh. I'm trapped in a swamp! Kit! Stop laughing...'

He came up beside her, slow and easy, folding his arms and eyes dancing with amusement as he took her in. 'Pride comes before a fall.'

'I haven't fallen.' Maddison tried to summon some shred of dignity, hard as it was to do when one foot was caught fast in a miniswamp, the other scrabbling for a firm foothold. Any minute now she was going to tumble and she'd be damned if she was going to fall in front of this man. Any man.

'Yet,' Kit pointed out helpfully.

'You could help me.'

'I could.' The laughter underpinned his words and she glared at him.

'Do you want me to beg?'

'Well…' He leaned in close and her breath hitched. His face was barely centimetres from hers, his shoulder close enough to grab, to hold on to, to bury herself in and let herself be saved.

She didn't need saving, did she? Just a helping hand.

'You could say *please*.'

Their eyes caught, held. His were alive with laughter, a teasing warmth curving his mouth, but behind the amusement was something hotter, something deeper, something straining to break through. And Maddison knew, with utter certainty, that all she needed to do was ask.

She hadn't asked for anything since she was six.

She glared, watching his amusement increase until a reluctant smile curved her lips. 'Please.'

'There, that wasn't so hard, was it?' Kit grasped

her hand and pulled. Maddison steadied herself against him, allowing him to take her weight as she heaved her foot free. It took a couple of tugs until, with a nasty squelch, the mud gave up and she stumbled forward, letting out a small yelp of alarm as she toppled, trying to get her balance.

'Easy, Maddison, I got you.'

He had. His arms were around her, steadying her, holding her up, and she allowed herself to be held, to be steadied. Just for a second. What harm could it do? What harm one moment of resting on someone else? One moment of needing someone else? Just a moment and then she would pull back, make some quip and carry on, ignoring the discomfort of her cold, damp boot and the sodden jeans because that was what Maddison Carter did, right? She carried on.

'Thanks.' Her breath was short and she inhaled, taking in the soap-fresh, wool scent of him, allowing her hands to remain on his waist as she pulled back, searching for the right kind of cheery smile that would put this moment behind them, behind her.

It was a lot to ask from a smile. And as she looked into his eyes any urge to laugh the moment off fell away as surely as the path plunged down towards the water, the sounds around drowned out by the blood rushing around her body, pulsing in her ears. All the amusement had drained out of his face, out of those blue eyes, now impossibly molten like sapphire forged in some great furnace. Instead she looked into the sharp planes of his face and saw want. She saw need. She saw desire.

For her.

'Kit?'

He didn't speak, his breathing ragged, his grip tightening on her shoulders. She should walk away; she needed to walk away because this, this wasn't planned. She had never let desire override her common sense before, and yet here she stood, making no move to reassert herself, passive in his grip.

The blood pounded faster, her stomach falling away, an almost unbearable ache pulsing in her breasts, beating insistently deep down in her very core. Maddison had always controlled every step of every seduction, when, how far, what, but now she had no power, no choice at all. Her body was taking over, need flaring up, overtaking sense, overtaking thought, overtaking everything.

She swayed towards him and his eyes flashed as they fixed on her mouth, hunger burning in their blue depths. Hunger for her.

For her. All of her.

Not just her body. She had laid herself bare before him, let him in to see all the nasty little corners she hid from everyone—and still he hungered. Maddison swayed closer still. His gaze was intoxicating and she could drink it in forever, bathe in the heat, helpless before his acceptance.

Kit released his grip on her shoulders, his hands moving slowly down her arms, each centimetre of her flesh blazing into life where his hands touched before burning with thwarted desire as his hands moved away. She was desperately trying to gulp in air, her chest tight with need.

Walk away, a small, sane part of her urged. *Walk away.*

But she had spent ten years being sane, ten years putting sense first, desire second. Didn't she deserve just a little time out? She was going to re-evaluate her plan anyway; she needed to explore all options, didn't she?

That was all this was. Exploring options. Because Kit didn't do love either. He was safe.

Maddison jumped as he reached out to cup her face, one finger tracing the curve of her mouth, a muscle beating insistently in his cheek. It took everything she had to hold his gaze, to stand there while his fingers explored the curve of her jaw, one tantalizing digit running slowly over her mouth, blazing a trail of fiery need. It was hard to breathe, hard to think, hard to stand still, hard not to step forward and grab him and make him fulfil that lazy promise. Her knees weakened as she watched the lines of his mouth, his eyes soften as they focused on her.

She looked up at him and allowed her mask to slip, just for a while. Allowed the desire and want and hope and need to shine through and as their eyes met she saw any resistance fall away.

She thought he would pull her close, go straight in for the kiss, but instead Kit moved back a little, one hand moving from her waist to the small of her back, leaving a trail of electric tingles as it oh-so slowly brushed over her body. Before today Maddison would have said that it would be impossible for anyone to feel anything under the thickness of her jacket but, like the princess lying on her tower of mattresses, every movement marked her. Claimed her.

'This crosses a line.' The words were so unexpected that Maddison didn't compute them at first. 'I should step away.' But he didn't.

'I think we already crossed that line.' Confidences, opening up emotionally, secret glances of shared amusement—to Maddison they were all far more intimate than mere sex. She suspected the same rang true for Kit. If there was a line to be crossed then they had walked blithely over it that day in the graveyard. Maybe even before then, when he had invited her out for a birthday drink. Maybe they had been heading here since then.

He closed his eyes briefly. 'Maybe you're right.' Then, only then did he step closer. Maddison hadn't appreciated quite how tall he was, how broad he was, how much coiled strength was hidden behind the quietly amused exterior until she was enfolded by him, in him. She had never allowed herself to feel fragile, delicate before, but the look in his eyes, the light, almost reverential touch, made her feel as if she were made of glass, infinitely precious. She shivered, heat and need running through her.

She slid her hands up his arms, allowing herself the time to appreciate the hard muscle under the thick material, until her hands met at the nape of his neck.

She stepped in, just that one bit closer so that leg was pressed against leg, her stomach against his taut abdomen, her breasts crushed against his chest. Desire rippled through her as the heat from his body penetrated her; she could barely raise her eyes to look at him, suddenly and unexpectedly shy. She was laying it all out there for him. What if she wasn't enough?

But the look in his eyes when she finally raised hers to meet his said it all and, emboldened, she pressed close and lifted her mouth to his. Softly at first, hesitant, and then as the kiss deepened she lost all reticence, holding him tighter, pulling him closer, revelling in the all-male taste of him, smell of him, feel of him. His hands hadn't moved, still just holding her close, burning where they touched her until she was almost writhing with the need for them to move, to have every inch lit up with that same sweet, intoxicating flame.

Maddison wound her hands through the soft hair at the nape of his neck, pulling him even closer, but it wasn't enough. The barriers of clothing, of skin too much. Impatient she slid her hands back down his torso, thrilling at the play of muscles under her hands, needing flesh on flesh.

'Maddison.' He broke away and she was instantly cold, even as he captured her hands in his, his thumbs caressing her palms. 'Slow down, lass. We shouldn't…'

'I…I…' She stumbled back, cheeks hot even as the rest of her shivered with an icy chill. 'You're right, we shouldn't…'

'Stay here,' he finished. 'We're a little exposed here on the public footpath.'

'Oh.' She smiled at him a little foolishly, blinking as she twisted in his embrace, aware for the first time in several long minutes of their surroundings. 'Yes.'

'We could get a hotel room, here. If you wanted,

that is. We'd still be back in time for the wedding. Only if you want to, though…'

Maddison put a finger on his mouth. 'I want to.'

'Good.' His voice was hoarse, ragged with need. 'I was very much hoping you would say that.'

The early-evening sun slanted in through the window, turning the red-gold of Maddison's hair flame-coloured. Kit pulled a strand of it through his fingers, the silky texture as smooth as her skin. He liked her hair like this, dishevelled, down, free, just as he liked her like this: soft, warm and drowsy.

What on earth had happened? One moment he was stomping up a steep hill, almost blind to the beauty all around him, taking little notice of the fresh air filling his lungs, trying not to mull over their conversation in the car, and the next moment… It hadn't just been the feel of her, soft and pliant in his arms as he'd pulled her free, it hadn't been the way she had looked, so different from her usual neat and tidy self in her jeans and jacket, hair falling out of its elegant twist, face rosy with the exercise. It had been more. Maybe they had been headed here all along.

Maybe it was the feelings she had roused in him in the car. Anger—not at her, *for* her. The abandoned child, the lonely girl, the jilted lover. She deserved more. But not just anger. She made him feel compassion, a need to possess her, protect her.

His mouth curled. As if he could protect anybody. And yet he wanted to, wanted to pull out a sword and challenge all comers, shield her from hurt.

'What are you thinking?' Maddison rolled over, the sheet pulled high, shielding her lithe body from his gaze. It was the body of someone with fierce amounts of control—slim, toned and smooth. It had been lots of fun helping her lose that control. Twice.

'That I hadn't expected to find myself here when we left London this morning.' That was an honest reply even if it wasn't all he was thinking.

She looked around and Kit followed her gaze, taking in, for the first time, the pink flowery walls, the heavy velvet curtains fringed with tassels, the huge variety of cushions and the shiny pine wardrobe. She smiled at him. 'No, I can imagine not. It's probably a little pink for your tastes.'

'We could have waited and found somewhere a little more boutiquey.' He didn't want to say romantic. This, whatever it was, wasn't about romance.

'No.' She slid a hand over his chest, a smug smile tilting the corners of her mouth as he inhaled sharply. 'This is perfect. Besides, I didn't want to wait.'

'No? Me neither.'

'Do you think the landlady bought it? The impromptu walking-weekend story?'

Kit allowed himself to twist another strand of that sunlit hair around a finger. 'Sure she did. I'm sure she's completely used to couples hammering at her door, throwing cash at her and disappearing upstairs.' The modest B & B had been the first place they had passed with a vacancies sign. It might not boast Egyptian cotton sheets, designer paint or expensive antiques, but it was clean and, most importantly, available. Neither of them had been prepared to wait for something more luxurious.

'I had a valid reason. I was covered with mud. I needed a bathroom.'

Kit whipped the sheet off, ignoring Maddison's squeals as she made a grab for it, and took a long, appraising look down at her legs. 'You still are.' He reluctantly let the sheet drop back down in response to her indignant tug and sank back down beside her. He could have feasted his eyes on her forever. 'You need a good wash. Want me to help?'

She pulled herself up on her forearm and looked down at him. 'Maybe. How good are you with a sponge?'

'Immensely talented,' he assured her and watched her eyes glaze over. 'Want to find out just how good I am?'

'Soon,' she promised him, slumping down onto him, her body hot against his skin. Kit shifted so that he was curled around her, his arm holding her tight, the heavy weight of her breast just under his hand. It had been so long since he had just lain with a woman, caught in that languorous twilight time between sex and the real world. The promise of pleasure still hanging, musky in the air, and yet sated enough to let the promise stand. For now. Maybe. He allowed his finger to circle around the tip of her breast, a light caress, a small possession as he burrowed his face into the sweet spot at the nape of her neck, tasting her skin one more time.

'Mmm…' Her sigh was all the encouragement he needed and he deepened the caress, his other hand sliding along her hip, across the flat plane of her belly, as he nibbled his way along her shoulder. 'Do we have to go to this wedding? Can't we stay here forever?'

Kit found the delicate spot at the top of her shoulder and tasted it, his tongue dipping into the hollow, following the line down towards the top of her other breast. Maddison shifted, allowing him access to her body, submissive under his gentle onslaught.

'I would much rather stay here.' He was taking his time, enjoying the quickening of her breath, her hands fisted in his hair. 'I am suddenly very fond of pink curtains.' But as he kissed his way down her body, sampling her slick, salty, satin skin, revelling in the knowledge that he was responsible for each moan, each cry, each movement, he knew that it was just a pipe dream.

Duty called him home. But tonight? Tonight was all about pleasure and Kit intended to make the most of every single second.

CHAPTER NINE

THE MORNING AFTER the night before. It wasn't usually a problem. After all, he always made his position completely clear before anything compromising began—no commitment, no emotional attachment, no expectations. Just two people hanging out, enjoying the moment. And if, in the end, the other person wanted more, well, his conscience was clear. He wasn't the one changing his mind.

But there had been no laying out of the rules this time. No clarity. Just an overwhelming need overriding sense, overriding thought. He could have taken her there and then on the hillside, mud and hikers forgotten. At least he'd had enough sense to call a temporary halt.

But not enough sense to halt it altogether.

Kit gripped the steering wheel until his knuckles whitened. Need meant weakness. Need meant attachment. He didn't do either. He only dated women he was in no danger of falling for. That was the rule.

Maddison Carter broke every rule.

But it wasn't as if she were after anything more serious either. Maddison had her heart set on her perfect marriage to the perfect guy who would give her the perfect family. And he was far from perfect.

Surely she knew that this, whatever it was, was just an interlude. She wouldn't want it to be anything more any more than he did.

Which in many ways made her the perfect woman.

Although following up a night of mind-blowing passion with a trip to the family home wasn't the best idea in the world. Even the most clear-headed of women would be forgiven for finding the signals confusing.

Maybe not just the women.

Kit turned his attention to the road ahead. Most people headed north from Loch Lomond, past Fort William, up into the deeper Highlands, but to get to Kilcanon Kit took an early turn away from the loch, dropping back down on to the long peninsula that would take them down, past the sea lochs to the coast. The road twisted and turned, climbing up into thickly forested heights where eagles soared before dropping back down to the loch side. Glasgow, just an hour and a half away, felt as remote as London or New York; a bustling city had nothing in common with this wild and natural beauty.

And Kilcanon was possibly the wildest and most beautiful part of all. The Buchanans' ancestral lands were at the very tip of the peninsula where land met sea. The road ahead was achingly familiar; here it was, the first glimpse of home. Every time it hit him anew, a sharp punch to his heart.

'There it is, Castle Kilcanon.' They were the first words either of them had spoken in the last hour and he slowed the car down so Maddison could look out at the sweep of water below, at the round grey castle dominating the landscape like a sentinel.

'That's your home?' She sat up straighter and peered down at the dark, rotund keep. 'Where's the flags on the turrets and the knights galloping over the drawbridge?'

'We don't keep the knights on a full retainer.'

The village spread out across the bay, the harbour home to several small boats bobbing on the sea, the castle on the other side of the bay. The weather had lifted a little and even though the grey of the sea met the grey of the sky on the horizon, the two blending into one, he could still see the craggy, green islands, some impossibly close, others mist-shielded ghosts.

'There's a lookout point. Can we stop?'

Kit didn't reply but he pulled over and sat there for a moment while she got out of the car and walked over to the railings, leaning over them while she took in the spectacular view. Once he'd have been hurrying her, eager to cover the last fifteen minutes' travel as the road wound down and round to the village, but not any more. Now he was glad of the opportunity to delay their arrival by even a few minutes.

In London he could push the memories away with work and play until all they could do was beat at his dreams, but as soon as he set foot in Kilcanon they would surround him, whispering ghosts reminding him that he was to blame. His eternal shame. His eternal punishment.

Maddison's hair was whipping around in the

breeze, the red-gold a vibrant contrast to the greens and blues surrounding her. He got out of the car and walked to the rail, leaning next to her. 'It's beautiful, isn't it?'

'Like nowhere else.'

'I'm sorry for yesterday.'

She slid a green-eyed glance over at him, the corners of her mouth curving into a playful smile, which caught him and held him. 'Why? I'm not.'

'It shouldn't have happened. I'm your boss and you were at a low point. I took advantage of you.'

'No, you cheered me right up. Made me feel desirable and wanted when I couldn't even look at myself without disgust.' She turned to face him, laying one slender hand over his. 'Look, Kit, it's all right. I'm not Camilla. I don't expect you to suddenly fall to one knee after one night together, no matter how amazing that night was. I know that's not what you are looking for and I…' She hesitated, lacing her fingers through his, her hand warm against the ice of his. 'I don't know what I want, not any more. It was all so clear-cut a few weeks ago. Even a few days ago.'

'Four children and a rich husband?'

She leaned into him with a playful shove. 'Yes. Well, marriage, a family, security. That is really important, although maybe I need to re-evaluate how I get there. But whatever happens I think I need to start living a little, not plan so much. So you are off the hook, nobody took advantage of anybody. It doesn't have to happen again, although,' she added, her fingers caressing his, 'I'm not saying that I'd mind if it did.'

'Remind me of that later,' he said softly and felt her quiver beside him.

He stared out at the sea—still today, tranquil. 'We used to take boats out over to the island, race them. Sails only, no motors allowed. Go fishing off the pier, kayak across the harbour. Everything was a competition, everything. Even love.'

'You miss him.' It wasn't a question.

'You have no idea how much. I don't feel it so much in London. He never visited me there—the city air was bad for his asthma—but here, by the sea, he was fine. Every time I come back it hits me again, that he's not here. And this evening I have to watch his wife marry someone else, as if Euan never existed.'

'It was three years ago, Kit. She's allowed to move on.'

'Maybe you're right.' He freed his hand from hers and moved to stand behind her, his arms around her waist holding on tight, allowing her to anchor him to the here and now. 'One of us should move on. We can't both hold an eternal vigil.'

'You are allowed to as well. It's what he would have wanted.'

If only she knew. He didn't think he would ever break free of the chains binding him to his guilt and grief—and even if he could, would he want to? Did he deserve to? Euan was dead and he was alive and nothing would ever change that.

'Come on.' He dropped a light kiss on her hair, breathing in the floral scent, glad that she was here in all her vibrancy and warmth, chasing away the shadows that dogged his every step. 'We have a family to meet and a wedding to attend. Ready?'

'Absolutely. Parents are my speciality. Lead the way.'

Kit took in a deep breath. There was no retreating now. But at least, this time, he wouldn't be alone.

* * *

Maddison wasn't quite as confident as the car swept up the long, gravelled drive to the castle. The gravel was grey like the thick stone blocks of the turrets. Grey like the sky above them, the sea behind them, and despite all her good intentions she shivered. 'Is that where you slept?' She tilted her head to look at the top of the keep, the windows narrow slits in the stone. It must be dark in there, dank. Her spine tingled as she imagined a small child, a mop of dark hair and huge blue eyes, sitting forlornly in a round, cheerless room.

'Oh, no, I was down in the dungeons. Kids are always better off behind bars. That's the family motto.' Kit was gripping the steering wheel a little tightly but his tone was teasing and the wink he gave her knowing.

'Of course you were, on a pallet of straw, a bucket in the corner.'

To Maddison's surprise the drive didn't end in front of the imposing entrance, but swept around the castle, finishing in a semicircle in front of an eye-wateringly large house situated on a slanting hill two hundred yards behind the castle. The house was built from the same grey stone as the keep but it seemed softer somehow, maybe because of the wisteria clambering over the front and upwards to the roof, maybe because of the elegant, tall towers flanking both sides, or maybe it was the three tiers of tall windows promising a light, airy interior, the stone in between them decorated with delicate ornamental stonework. Either way, despite its size, it made a more believable—and more comfortable—home than the ancient, thick-walled castle.

Kit braked the car and pointed up to the top floor. 'The nursery floor was up there. Euan, Bridget and I all had rooms up there, along with the playroom.'

She barely took in his words, her mouth open in utter shock. 'It's…it's huge!' Somehow the grand old house was more imposing than any castle could be. Twisting around in her seat, Maddison could see how the ground had been cleverly landscaped so that the keep hid the house from prying eyes and yet the house itself had an uninterrupted view, over smooth green lawns, right down to the sea. Behind the house lawns rose in wide, flower-covered terraces up into the hillside, hints of arbours, patios and summer houses hidden just out of view. She turned back to Kit and eyed him accusingly. 'I can't believe you let me think that you still lived in there.'

He grinned. 'It's a common misconception but the keep's been empty for years. By all accounts it was always cold and uncomfortable and our eighteenth-century ancestors were too nesh to keep shivering in there. With the Jacobite rebellion over they didn't need such thick walls and so they built the big house, as it's still known. Only the old castle gets the courtesy of being Castle Kilcanon, the ancestral home of the Clan Buchanan.' He deepened his voice as he said the last words, sounding more like a documentary maker than a son returning home.

'The big house?' Maddison had never quite got the British art of understatement. The house in front of her made the estates of her college friends seem small—and tacky—even though she had visited homes covering many more acres. She instinctively knew there would be no cinema rooms or bowling alleys here, no infinity pools or gyms. This was real class, real old money. She had no idea how to fake this kind of lifestyle. How to fit in.

For the first time in many years doubt clouded her mind. She shivered again as a raven landed on top of the keep, a foreboding omen.

'Kit!' Maddison had no more time to panic as the huge front door was flung open and a pretty girl in her early twenties ran down the imposing front steps. She was casually dressed in an old sweater and jeans, her dark red hair scooped back and not a hint of make-up on the creamy face, liberally strewn with becoming freckles. Maddison pulled her cashmere jumper down, smoothing it with shaking hands, doubting her outfit. Was it too put together? Artificial?

'Kit! You're home! I can't believe you left it till now. Mum has been spitting feathers. She was convinced you'd let her down and find an excuse not to come. Not that I blame you. If it wasn't a three-line whip I would be far away from here. It sounds utterly dreary.'

'Hey, Bridge.' Kit was out of the car before the girl got to them and reached down, scooping her up and swinging her round. Maddison's chest squeezed. She would give anything to have someone greet her with such uninhibited joy. 'I have plenty of time. The wedding doesn't start until five.'

'I know.' The younger girl pulled a face. 'Evening candlelit ceremony and black tie. So tacky. I blame Angus.'

'I doubt Angus had much of a say,' Kit said drily.

Maddison got out of the car, her legs stiff and awkward as she walked around to meet them, her throat dry and chest tight. She had thought she didn't care what Kit's family made of her, but she wanted this warm-faced girl who so obviously adored Kit to like her. To think her worthy.

Worthy of what? she reminded herself. *One night does not make a future. And you don't want that, remember?*

But it was hard to remember just what she did want as Kit put a steadying arm around her and led her forward. 'Maddison, this is my little sister, Bridget. Bridge, this is Maddison.'

'It's nice to meet you at last.' Bridget held out her hand. 'We've spoken on the phone so often I feel that I know you already but it's much nicer face-to-face. We'll have to have a real gossip straight away and you can tell me all about what a tyrant Kit is and fill me in on all his secrets.' She threw a speaking glance at her brother. 'There's tea and scones waiting in the drawing room. And no, you can't escape. Behave.'

'We should have dawdled more on the way.' Kit squeezed Maddison's shoulder. 'Ready? Some trials involve dragons and daring rescues, others golden apples and races. My mother conducts trial by small talk. It's deadly, it's terrifying but it's possible to survive.'

Bridget elbowed him. 'Don't scare her, idiot. It's not that bad,' she added to Maddison. 'At least the scones are good.'

When Maddison visited her college friends' homes, finding a valid reason to be free from her fictional family over Christmas or Thanksgiving, she rarely saw their parents. She'd arrive at some spacious, interior-decorated-to-within-an-inch-of-its-life mansion, be whisked off to an en-suite room bigger than any apartment she'd ever lived in and then spend the next few days in the kind of pampered bubble the set she chose to run with considered normal. Food was pulled without consideration from cavernous fridges, or prepared by smiling, silent maids. Parents rushed in with platitudes and compliments before rushing back out again to the club, to work, to a party or a personal-training session. Maddison knew how to smile, compliment prettily and make the right kind of impression to be invited back.

But scones and a small-talk-stroke-interrogation in a house older than an entire state was another thing entirely. She leaned a little more heavily against Kit as they approached the front door. The big house might lack a moat but stepping over the threshold felt as final as watching the drawbridge close up behind her.

Bridget led them into a huge hallway dominated by closed, heavy wooden doors interspersed with portraits of stern-looking men in kilts surveying the landscape and even sterner-looking ladies in a variety of intricate hairstyles. Nearly every portrait featured some kind of massive dog and a gloomy-looking sea. A wide staircase started halfway down the hall, sweeping imperiously up towards the next floor with a dramatic curve, the carved wooden bannister shining like a freshly foraged chestnut. She swallowed as her eyes passed over tarnished gilt mirrors and ancient-looking vases.

'This is all very formal.' Kit squeezed Maddison's shoulder. 'Bridge must be trying to make an impression on you. Usually we come in through the back.'

'I didn't think Maddison would want to pick her way through thirty pairs of mismatched wellies, twenty broken fishing rods, enough waterproofs to clothe an army and the dogs' toys,' Bridget said. She flashed a shy smile at Maddison. 'But Kit's right, the front door is usually just for guests. It takes far too long to open it, for one thing, and there's nowhere to dump your coat, for another.'

Maddison couldn't imagine wanting to dump her coat. The air was as chilly as a top New York law firm's offices, only this wasn't status-boosting air conditioning, it was all too natural. 'It's lovely,' she said. 'Very…' She looked up at the nearest portrait for inspiration. The sitter was scowling, his grey, pigtailed wig low on his brow, his sword angled menacingly. 'Very old.'

'The bannister is good for sliding on,' Kit said. 'And when the parents went out we used to practise curling on these tiles. There's no heating at all in the hallway so in winter they get pretty icy.'

Maddison had no clue what he was talking about so she just smiled. But she knew one thing for sure. She couldn't get carried away here, couldn't change her game plan, couldn't hope that whatever had sparked into life yesterday was real. She would never belong in a place like this; there were limits to even her self-deception. So she might as well relax and enjoy it for what it was. A fun interlude before she went home to New York and decided what she was going to do with the rest of her life.

The problem was that her original prize wasn't looking quite as golden as it used to. It wasn't that she didn't want security; she did. She still needed it just as she needed air and water. She still wanted children who teased each other the way Kit and Bridget were, children who were raised with the kind of love that Kit seemed to take for granted and with the same opportunities. She just wanted a little bit more.

She wanted the full package. Security, love and respect. And by raising the stakes she might have just doomed her entire quest to failure.

CHAPTER TEN

THERE WAS SOMETHING incredibly seductive about watching a woman getting dressed for a big occasion. The concentration on her face as she twisted her hair up just so, the way she slid the small point of an earring into her lobe, the purse of her mouth as she painted it an even deeper red.

The way she rolled on her underwear, a subtle mixture of practicality and romance, a little like its wearer. The black silky bra designed to show off her shoulders in the thinly strapped dress, the wispy knickers Kit had to drag his eyes away from because they really, really didn't have time. Yet.

Maddison was wearing the same dress she had worn to the opera, a simple knee-length black dress with a white strip around her waist, echoed by a wider band at the bottom of the dress. The invitation had specified Black Tie and Kit knew that the other female guests would be going all out. Maddison, with her knot of red-gold hair and the pearls in her ears, would probably be the simplest-dressed woman in the room—and the most beautiful, he realized with a twist of his stomach.

His mother had put them in one of the suites, two bedrooms and a shared bathroom, a sign she was unsure of their romantic status. Kit shared her uncertainty—common sense told him to walk away quickly while it was still possible to extricate himself with grace, but his body told him something very different.

Right now his body was winning.

Which had the advantage of both distracting him from the forthcoming wedding and lessening the pain of Euan's absence. So he would let his body win—for now.

'You're looking thoughtful.' Maddison moved towards him, her gait slower, sexier in her high heels, and laid a reassuring hand on his shoulder. 'Let me get that for you.' And with practised ease she adjusted his bow tie. 'Very dapper. Are you worrying about tonight?'

'Not really. I was just admiring how you managed my mother earlier. It was like watching two fencers spar.' His mother's patented brand of tea and interrogation usually either froze her opponents into stunned silence or cracked them open until they had spilled every secret. Not many managed to parry and block with the same deft touch Maddison had shown.

'I had quite a lot of fun. She's a formidable opponent. I had no idea what to call her, though— Mrs Buchanan? The housekeeper says My Lady but I'm not sure I could say that and keep a straight face. I'd feel like a housemaid in Downton.'

'I'm sorry, I should have warned you how absurdly formal it can be here. My father is the Viscount of Kilcanon and my mother is Lady of Kilcanon but in speech you say Lord and Lady Buchanan. Locally, though, they are mostly known as the Laird and Lady. I know,' he said apologetically as her forehead creased in puzzlement. 'It's all a little feudal.'

'Aren't Laird and Lord the same thing?'

'No, not really. Angus, the lucky groom...' Kit cast a look at the clock on the wall, relieved to see they still had an hour before they had to leave '…he's the local laird in Kameskill because he's the biggest landowner, but it's an honorary title. If he sold the estate the title would pass with it. If we sold this estate then Dad still stays a viscount.'

'So wait, do you have a cool title? Do I get to call you Sir?'

Kit sighed. He hated this part. 'Both Bridge and I are Honourables, but neither of us use it,' he admitted. 'And now Euan's gone I'm Master of Kilcanon.'

'Master? How very dominant of you.'

He matched her grin. 'Remind me to show you later…'

'Chicken…' she said softly and his blood began to pound at the challenge.

'Unfortunately we have been summoned to a pre-wedding drink with my family, but wait until we return and I'll show you who is master.'

'I can hardly wait…' She sashayed before him but stepped aside as she reached the door so that Kit could go first.

He touched her shoulder. 'Worried about the dogs? I can get Morag to lock them away.' One of the family pets had wandered into the drawing room when they were having tea and Maddison had paled significantly and made no move towards it, retreating a little when it had stalked nearer her.

'No.' But she didn't sound at all convincing. 'Honestly, I'm fine. It's just they are really *big*.'

'Another thing I should have warned you about. I forget not everyone has grown up with dogs the size of small ponies.'

'Small ponies? Are you kidding? I think they would outrank a medium pony and maybe even a large one.' She was smiling but there was a look of trepidation in her eyes and he decided he'd better keep the dogs away from her. They were very sweet tempered but fifty kilograms of dog could be intimidating to even the most ardent of dog lovers. 'Still,' she said, with that same game smile on her face, 'I guess a smaller dog would get lost in a house this size.'

'There's still a corgi or two somewhere in the west wing and a dachshund stuck in the tower,' he agreed straight-faced and was rewarded with a moment of puzzlement before she glared at him and stalked out of the room.

As was customary, drinks were in the library

and, sure enough, when Kit ushered Maddison into the book-lined room two of the family's prized deerhounds were flaked out on a tattered old red rug in front of the fire. One of them raised a lazy head in their direction and Maddison tensed, her arm rigid under his hand, before the dog flopped back down, too tired from its day to properly investigate the newcomer.

Maddison swallowed. 'I feel even more Downton than ever,' she said, and Kit tried to see the familiar room through her eyes: the oak panels, the huge leaded windows, the tall bookcases, which needed a ladder to reach the top shelves, the leather chesterfield and the old walnut bureau where his father conducted his business just as his grandfather had before him and so on back into the mists of time.

'It's all too dusty to be truly Downton,' Kit whispered. 'No butler either, just Morag, and she never bobs a curtsey and is always gone by six.'

'Kit.' His attention was called away by his father's curt tones. Lord Buchanan was standing by the fireplace, a glass of single malt in one hand. Looking at him was like looking into a portrait in the attic, Kit in thirty years' time. Not that Kit often looked straight at his father. How could he when he was responsible for so much loss? For the lines creasing his father's forehead and the shadows in his mother's eyes?

He ushered Maddison forward. She, he noted, was still keeping a wary eye on the dogs. 'Dad, good to see you. This is Maddison Carter, my very able assistant, who very kindly agreed to accompany me this weekend. Maddison, my father.'

His father nodded briefly at Maddison but didn't speak and Kit was grateful when Bridget pulled her over to the sofa she was sitting on, thrusting a glass of champagne into his hand as she did so. Conversations with his father were rarely comfortable and he'd rather not have a witness.

This was the problem with bringing anyone home. They saw too much.

Lord Buchanan stiffened as he glanced at the champagne Kit was holding, swirling his own whisky as if in challenge. 'It's good to see you still know the way home, son.'

It was going to be like that, was it? He wasn't

going to rise, he wasn't... 'Luckily there's always satnav.' Okay, he was going to rise a little.

His father didn't respond to the jibe. 'Whatever it takes.'

Kit looked over at Maddison. She seemed comfortable enough sitting between Bridget and his mother. As he'd expected his mother was dressed traditionally in a long blue dress, a sash of the family tartan over her shoulder fastened with a sapphire brooch. Bridget was less traditional and tartan free, but still in a floor-length dress in a sparkly material. Maddison didn't seem bothered though; she had that same self-possessed look on her face that she usually wore in the office.

Maddison looked up and caught his eye and for one all-too-brief moment they were the only people in the room. Kit's heart hitched, missing a beat. What would it be like under different circumstances, bringing a girl like Maddison home to meet the family?

His father followed his gaze over and looked at Maddison speculatively before transferring his gaze to his son. His lip curled. 'What are you wearing? A kilt not good enough for you any more?'

Kit tore his eyes away from Maddison and looked down at his neatly tailored tuxedo, shrugging. The last time he'd worn his kilt had been at Euan's funeral; he'd managed to avoid any formal occasion in Scotland since then, wearing a black tuxedo when necessary in London.

'I wore the kilt to Eleanor's last wedding.' He saw his mother look up at that and remorse stabbed him at his bitter words. 'I just couldn't,' he added in a more conciliatory tone.

But it wasn't enough. His father shook his head. 'You get more Londonified by the day. You're needed here. It's time you shouldered your responsibilities and…'

And so it started, just as it did every time he spoke to his father. Every conversation they had had since the funeral. The same words, the same tone, the same message. He was needed here. He was responsible for this mess and he damn well better clean it up.

Didn't he know it? And that was why he couldn't be the son his father wanted. How could he come here and just take Euan's place as if he deserved it? Step into his dead brother's shoes?

'I have shouldered them. I can just as easily watch you ignore every suggestion I make from London.'

His father fixed him with a glare from eyes so familiar it was like looking in a mirror. 'You'll be responsible for this place one day and God knows I'll make sure you know how to run it.'

Admit it, you wish I had died instead. Kit took a deep breath, swallowing the bitter words back. 'Did you look at diversifying the cloth making and selling directly to the public like I suggested? How about setting up our own distillery? Doing up the holiday cottages?' His father remained silent and Kit threw his hands in the air. 'I did business plans for all those projects, found the right people. If you're not interested...'

His father interrupted, red in the face. 'You just want to change things. You have no interest in the traditions of the place.'

Kit was suddenly tired. 'I do. And that's why I want to make sure Kilcanon can remain sustainable.'

'Sustainable...' His father gesticulated and as

he did so he let go of his glass. It fell in horrifying slow motion, whisky flying from it in a sweet-smelling amber shower, until the one-hundred-year-old crystal bounced off the sharp edge of the marble hearth, shattering into hundreds of tiny, razor-like shards. Everyone shouted out, the women jumping to their feet, Kit and his father taking an instinctive step back and both dogs bounding up from their fireside bed in a panicked tangle of howls and whines.

'Iain!'

'Damn fool, look what you made me do.'

'I'll get a cloth and a dustpan…' Bridge, of course, sidling out of the room as fast as she could; unusually for a Buchanan, she hated confrontation.

'Dad, have you cut yourself?'

'Oh, Iain, really. The car will be here in twenty minutes. Come with me. I'll fix you up. I told you to control your temper. No wonder Kit never comes home and I'm sure Maddison will never want to come here again. What must she be thinking?' His mother's voice faded away as she steered his father out of the room and up the stairs.

Kit turned to Maddison, an apology ready on his lips, but it remained unuttered. She wasn't looking at him; all her attention was on one of the dogs, still whimpering by the fire. He touched her arm to reassure her but it wasn't fear he saw on her face, it was concern.

'The dog...' she half whispered. 'I think it's hurt.'

Sure enough, although Heather had retreated to the doorway, her tail and ears down but otherwise unhurt, Thistle had barely moved from the old red rug that had been the dogs' library bed for as long as Kit could remember.

'Thistle?' Heedless of the glass still scattered everywhere, Kit dropped to his knees beside the dog, still sitting whining by the fire, one paw held at a drooping angle. Thistle's ears trembled and his tail gave a pathetic thump, his huge dark eyes staring pleadingly at Kit. 'Are you hurt, old boy?' He extended a gentle hand towards the paw but Thistle moved it back, his ears flattening as he let out a low growl. 'Come on,' Kit said coaxingly but the next growl was a little louder.

Heather, still at the door, began to pace, her tail still drooping. Kit glanced up at Maddison.

This must be her worst nightmare. She was wary enough of the huge dogs as it was—one doing a lion impression and the other growling like a bear was unlikely to reassure her. 'Now I understand the point of corgis. A little easier to wrestle into submission! I don't want to hurt him further but I do need to see that paw.'

She was pale, her lips almost colourless, and there was a faint tremor in her fingers, but she made an attempt at a smile and crouched beside him. 'I think one of us needs to reassure him while the other examines his paw.'

'So which end do you fancy, claws or teeth?' Kit wasn't being serious, he was intending to send her to get some water and some help, but to his amazement she laid a gentle hand on Thistle's head, slowly rubbing the sweet spot behind his ears and crooning to him in a low voice.

'Who's a brave bear? I know. I know it hurts but you need to let us look at it.' Her voice and the slow caress of her hand were almost hypnotic and Thistle gave a deep sigh, slumping down, his massive head on her knee. Maddison continued to talk to him, gentle words of comfort and love, one hand still rubbing his ear, the other sliding along the dog's shoulder until she was supporting the dog's paw. Thistle gave a quick jerk in pain and then lay still again.

With a quick glance at Maddison to make sure she was all right, Kit slowly and carefully turned the great paw over. The three dark pads, usually velvety soft, were damp, the fur between matted with blood. 'I think he's got glass in there,' Kit said as quietly as he could. 'Are you okay down there while I get some tweezers, water and some antibacterial cream?'

He rose to his feet as she nodded, and backed towards the door, one hand reassuring Heather, who had stopped pacing to sit staring anxiously at her litter mate still half lying in Maddison's lap.

And Maddison… Kit's breath caught in his throat. The fire lit her up, turning the strawberry-blonde hair gold, casting a warm glow over her pale skin. She was unmoving, her face set, partly through concentration, partly to hide the fear he knew she felt. With the blood from Thistle's paw on her hands and soaking into the white hem of her dress, she looked like Artemis straight from the hunt. Fiery, blood-stained war-rior queen.

His heart gave a painful lurch, as if the ice en-casing it were cracking. But that was okay. It was thick enough to handle a few cracks. He was in no danger of melting anytime soon.

'I can't wear this.' Maddison plucked at the long skirt and stared at Kit's mother anxiously. 'Re-ally my, I mean, Lady Buchanan.' She hated that she'd stumbled over the words but what the fricking heck? She'd never thought she'd need to know the right way to address a viscountess before.

If Kit's mother *was* a viscountess. Was that even a thing?

'Don't be silly,' Lady Buchanan said briskly. 'Your own dress is covered in blood.' Her mouth twisted in an unexpectedly vulnerable move-ment. 'Attending my son's widow's marriage is hard enough. We'll be the victims of more than enough vulgar gossip without bringing the bride of Dracula with us.'

'That's a good point. I promise I'll try not to spill on this.' Maddison eyed her reflection nervously. There was an awful amount of fabric to keep clean and away from candles, especially in the floating skirt and the long, see-through chiffon sleeves. Apart from the neckline. There wasn't nearly enough material there; she swore she could see her navel if she looked hard enough.

'It's just so nice to see it being worn again.' Lady Buchanan's eyes were wistful as she rearranged the beading that encircled the low, low neckline and looped higher up Maddison's chest like a necklace. 'Bridget won't touch any of my clothes and dear Eleanor, well, it wasn't really her style. I wore this the first time I met Iain, at Hogmanay right here in this house. I wore a cape over it so my father didn't make me get changed. It was a little risqué back in the seventies.'

It was still risqué as far as Maddison was concerned. But the mint green suited her colouring and besides… 'It's vintage Halston,' she breathed reverentially. 'A design classic. It's an honour to wear it.' Even if it wasn't standard wedding attire, Maddison suspected she'd have got less attention in the blood-stained dress.

'It's the least I can do. You were so quick-thinking and brave, helping poor Thistle like that. Kit thinks he has all the glass out but Morag is going to stay late and wait in for the vet just in case. I'd have stayed myself but it's important we attend this wedding with our heads high. Never let it be said that the Buchanans retreat from a challenge although...' Her voice broke off, her eyes so sad that Maddison wished she could give her a hug.

But could she hug a viscountess without permission or was that some kind of treason? And besides, she wasn't confident that she could lean forward in this dress *and* stay in it.

'It was nothing. Thistle was very brave.'

'It's not just Thistle you're helping though. Kit seems different, less brittle. Happier. To see my boy smile I'd hand over one hundred dresses.'

Maddison tried not to squirm as the sincere words washed over her. It couldn't be denied that she was making Kit happy, but not in the way Lady Buchanan meant. Kit's mother was talking about his heart, not his body. One she was happily familiar with, the other she suspected had been locked away several years ago.

And she was pretty sure he had no intention

of handing over the key. Even if he did, was she the right person to unlock it? What did she know of families and castles and long-standing traditions? She didn't belong in a place like this; she never would. Coming here was a reality check she badly needed. She could enjoy Kit's company, share his bed—but she would never be the right person to share his life. Cinderella might have made the move from the fireside to the castle, but the trailer was a step too far down. And pretend as she might, she would never shed her past completely.

CHAPTER ELEVEN

'HAVE I TOLD you that you look…?'

'Inappropriately dressed?' Maddison supplied, resisting the temptation to hoick the sides of her dress together back across her chest. She'd give anything for a pin right now.

'I was going to say hot. Definitely hotter than the bride.'

'That's always my goal at weddings.' Maddison stepped even further into the shadows at the back of the hall. 'At least it's so gloomy in here I'm hoping no one knows this is actual skin on show and assumes there's some kind of nude-coloured top going on.'

'When Eleanor decided on candlelight I don't think she took into consideration just how much light these old banqueting halls need. It feels more like Halloween than a wedding.'

'She looked beautiful though. Eleanor.' Maddison hadn't expected the surge of jealousy when the bride, a mere thirty-five minutes late, had glided ethereally down the aisle. She hadn't known what to expect from Kit's first and only love but it hadn't been the dark-eyed, dark-haired, diminutive beauty who had floated along in a confection of lace. No wonder both brothers had fallen for her, chosen her over their sibling bond.

Even her voice was beautiful, chiming out her vows in clear bell-like tones. Maddison, hidden in a back corner, shrank into herself, uneasily aware of just how gaudy her own brilliant colouring could look, how brash her own decisive tones.

'She always looks beautiful.' But Kit didn't sound admiring or wistful. Just dismissive. 'It's all she has, really. She's good at turning those big eyes on you and making you think she matters, but when I look back at our year together I can't remember much that she said of any substance. Still, Angus wants someone to look good when he's hosting parties and to pop out an heir or two so they'll both be happy.'

Maddison winced as his words sliced into her. That was her plan, wasn't it? Find someone who wanted a compatible partner to keep the home fires burning, be a corporate wife and raise the kids. That was her goal. Planned for, prepared for, ready for... Maddison looked from Kit, slightly dishevelled yet absurdly sexy in his tux, to Angus, sweaty, balding, one arm proprietorially round his bride, and swallowed, a lump in her throat. It didn't seem such a laudable goal any more.

Kit followed her gaze and huffed out a short laugh. 'Good Lord, Angus is already half-cut. Some wedding night this is going to be.' As he spoke Eleanor looked round and caught sight of Kit. Was that regret in those huge eyes? Regret for turning him down the first time? Or regret for not hooking him in the second?

'I don't think I can stand much more of this. We've definitely done our duty,' Kit whispered into her ear, his breath heating the sensitive skin, sending tingling, hopeful messages straight to the pit of her stomach, to her knees, so she wanted to melt into his voice, his strength, his touch. 'Fancy finding a real party?'

Normally Maddison would be in her element in a gathering like this. Kit had pointed out several titles, a brace of millionaires and a group of heirs and a wedding was the ideal place to start up a conversation with any eligible man. Even though she wasn't looking for a UK-based guy, a picture of Maddison and the heir to an oil fortune posted somewhere Bart would see should be very satisfying. But somehow in the last couple of weeks she had lost any interest in impressing Bart.

Kit was right. Maybe he had been interested in her the way she was originally and her attempt to be his perfect woman had bored him. And if he hadn't been, then would she really want to build a whole life on a pretence? 'Sure. Only…' Maddison gestured at her dress. 'Where on earth can I go dressed like this? Studio 54?'

'You'll be fine where we're going. No one will raise an eyebrow.' He stopped to consider, his gaze travelling slowly down the deep vee in her neckline. Neckline? Navel line. 'Okay. They might raise *an* eyebrow, both eyebrows. But if we're lucky you might score us free drinks all night and they'll crown you harbour queen.'

'Harbour queen? Is that a thing?'

'It definitely should be. What do you say?'

Maddison cast a quick look around the high-ceilinged, grey stone room. It had been decorated to within an inch of its five-hundred-year-old life, the walls draped in a deep red fabric, the floor covered in matching carpeting, huge vases of red and white flowers dotted in every alcove, on every table. A violin quartet were playing traditional music high up in the minstrels' gallery and food and drink circulated freely. But even with the opulent decor, with the candles glittering from the candelabra on the wall and the gigantic chandelier, the gloom penetrated and, she shivered, the temperature remained chilly.

'It seems kind of rude to just go.'

'You're right. Besides, the ceilidh will start soon and in that dress you're going to be every man here's partner of choice. Think your neckline will stay intact after a round of Gay Gordons?'

Maddison had no idea what a Gay Gordon or a ceilidh was but the suggestive glint in Kit's eye warned she might be better off not finding out. 'As I was saying, it seems kind of rude to just leave but there's so many people here I guess no one will miss us.'

His smile was pure wickedness. 'I think you've made the right choice.'

It took a while before they actually left. Kit wanted to make sure he had fulfilled his role as Master of Kilcanon and switched on the professional facade so familiar from the office as he circulated the room, shaking hands, kissing cheeks and making easy small talk as if he had been born to it.

Which of course he had.

The whirlwind charm offensive finished at the bridal party with kisses for the bride, her mother and bridesmaids and a hearty, back-slapping conversation with the bemused-looking groom before they finally slipped out of the room.

'No one will be able to accuse me of not giving the wedding my full blessing,' Kit said as they collected their coats, heading out of a small side door into the cool, dark evening rather than making their way back along the long formal hallway to the gigantic front door.

'I think you scared the groom. He looked like he thought you were going to kiss him at one point.' Eleanor had kept that same cool half-smile on her lips, Maddison had noticed, but there had been a hint of hurt in her eyes. What had she been expecting? Pistols at dawn?

They made their way around the rectangular building, their way lit by small hidden lights on the path, the sounds of merriment floating out of the opened windows into the evening air. Angus's house wasn't as old as Castle Kilcanon or as elegant as the big house but it made up in size and ostentation what it lacked in authenticity. Surely it didn't need quite so many towers?

Looking up, Maddison saw the darkest sky she'd laid eyes on since she had first moved to New York four years ago, a deep, velvety blackness studded with stunningly bright flickers of light. Normally this level of darkness would panic her but Kit had tight hold of her hand, as if he knew that she might react.

Maddison's pulse began to throb. Nobody had anticipated her needs, her moods in such a long time. She squeezed his hand thankfully and breathed in deep. The air was so pure, so fresh it almost hurt her city lungs, better than any perfume or room spray.

The path brought them out onto the long, sweeping driveway and their taxi waited at the end, beyond the imposing wrought-iron gates, the modern equivalent of a drawbridge. Maddison gave a heartfelt sigh of relief when she saw the headlights; her shoes were pinching, her toes were cold and her bones so chilled she wasn't sure she'd ever feel warm again.

It was the same driver who had taken them to the wedding. Maddison suspected he was probably the only taxi driver in Kilcanon, which gave her little comfort as he set off at a white-knuckled fast pace down the dark and twisting road. Kit settled back in his seat, silent as the car flashed through the night, covering the three miles in what surely must be record time but, as the car raced to the top of the hill and the first lights in the village could be seen in the dip below, Kit reached out and took her hand again, lacing his fingers through hers with a strong, steady pressure.

There was an intimacy about holding hands in the dark that went beyond the kisses, the caresses, the passion they had shared yesterday. Maddison swallowed, a lump burning in her throat. She shouldn't get used to this. He didn't do love, remember? Neither did she.

Only she wasn't quite as sure about that any more. She wasn't sure she would swap this taxi for the fanciest of limos, the man next to her for a Kennedy, last night for a lifetime of security. Maddison stared out the window at the darkness. In that case what did she want—and was she in danger of trading all she'd ever dreamed of for heartbreak?

Maddison had expected that they would head either to a private house or to the whitewashed grand hotel that dominated the corner where the main road hit the harbour, but the taxi drove straight on, bypassing the hotel, bypassing the grand Victorian villas looking out to sea, bypassing the small and friendly pub she'd noticed earlier. The moon was high and full, laying out a silvery path along the dark sea, and Maddison had an urge to follow it and see what strange land it took her to.

Finally, once they had swept right around the harbour road and reached a small row of cottages, the taxi pulled up. Maddison opened her door, gratefully gulping in some air, her stomach unsettled by the fast and twisting journey. She looked around, confused. In front of her a door stood open but the inner door was closed and the windows tightly shuttered, although she could hear music coming from within.

'Where are we?'

Kit had walked around to join her. He extended a hand to help her out of the car and gestured towards the door. 'This is where the locals come to play. Ready?'

Maddison cast a long, covetous look back along the harbour wall towards the hotel, shining beacon-like, a promise of hospitality, warmth and civilization. 'Sure.'

'Good.' And Kit opened the shut inner door and ushered her inside.

The first thing that hit her was the noise. Or the lack of it. Just like any good western, the room came to an abrupt silence as she was propelled through the door to stand gaping on the threshold. The second thing to strike her was the simplicity: whitewashed walls, wooden tables and stools, a dartboard and pool table visible in the adjoining room. The third thing she noticed was the heat, the glorious, roaring heat that came from a generous log fire.

The fourth and final thing Maddison realized

was that, if she had been inappropriately dressed for a wedding, here, in a room full of jeans, plaid shirts and sweaters, she looked like a bordello girl amidst the cowboys. Only more underdressed.

'Kit!' The man behind the bar broke the stunned silence and slowly, like dominoes falling into each other, the room came back to life. Conversations restarted, darts were thrown and through the alcove Maddison could hear the unmistakable clink of pool balls being lined up. She hadn't played for years. Nice girls didn't hang around pool tables. Another thing she missed.

'All right, Paul.'

Maddison was barely listening as the two men launched into a series of 'how are you?'s and 'what have you been up to?'s. The accents in the little bar were stronger than any she had come across before and it was easier to let the voices wash over her than try and make sense of the conversation, which, from what she could glean, revolved around fishing anyway. A pint of something amber was handed to her and she took it. Beer. She didn't drink beer, not any more, not since high school, an illicit keg on the beach wearing her boyfriend's varsity jacket even though she wasn't cold. Because it marked her. Marked her as an insider.

She sniffed the beer cautiously, breathing in the nostalgia of the tangy, slightly metallic aroma, then took a sip. It was delicious. She took another.

'There's a seat by the fire.' Kit had finished his conversation and turned to her. 'Fancy it?'

'For now.' She smiled slowly, licking the slight froth from her lip as she did so, and watched Kit's eyes darken to navy blue. 'But later I want to play pool.'

Was this what a relationship was? Discovering new parts of someone, being surprised by them, delighted by them, in new ways every day. Eleanor had always been the same—cool, collected, affectionate but in a way that made it clear she was in control. He saw it now for what it was: a way to keep him in line, wanting more. And he'd never allowed anyone else close enough to find out what one facet of their personality was like, let alone several.

But here he was. And here Maddison was. The

hardworking assistant, smooth and reliable. The clue solver, her quick brain jumping ahead, unabashedly delighted when she was first with an answer. The opera lover, enthralled by the music, lost in a world he couldn't touch. The warrior, conquering her fear to help a creature in pain. The lover, tender, demanding, exciting, yielding.

And now—the pool shark. It wasn't just the dress distracting him; she had borrowed a T-shirt from Paul, the barman, to even up the odds somewhat—there wasn't a man in here who could have played her in that dress and survived. It wasn't the adorable way she bit her lip as she focused on the cue ball or the way she caressed the tip of the cue while sizing up her shot, although both of those gave her a definite advantage. No, the truth was she was very, very good. Or lucky. He hadn't decided which.

She was also more than a little drunk, having moved on to whisky. She had unwittingly committed sacrilege and asked for a blended whiskey but Kit had jumped in to change her order to the local single malt, although he had allowed it to be poured on ice. Her face at the first sip had had the entire bar in stitches but she had persevered a little too well—was that her second glass or her third?

'Another round?'

Was she talking about whisky or the pool? Kit wasn't sure he could take either. 'I wouldn't mind some air first,' he suggested.

Maddison narrowed her eyes at him, reminding Kit irresistibly of a cat in her unwavering focus. 'Scared?'

'Terrified. My reputation may never recover.' Truth was some of his shots had gone awry because she was so damn adorable when she was competitive, but he wasn't going to admit that. It would just make her win all the more complete.

'Okay. Air and then I whip your ass again. Deal?'

'Deal.'

He steered her out of the door, realizing as he hit the street that she wasn't the only one feeling the effects of the whisky. Kit was mellower, calmer than he had felt in a long time. The cool night air was a welcome relief from the heat of the bar, the sound of the waves soothing after the laughter, loud talk and music pumping through the two small rooms. Kit reached for Maddison's hand, breathing in a sigh of relief as the peace hit him.

Only for the peace to retreat as the past roared in to engulf him once again. A past he would never be free of, not here, no matter whose hand he held, how much whisky he sank. No matter how much he tried.

'Hey, are you okay?'

Kit loosened his grip on Maddison's hand with a muttered apology. 'I thought this time was different, this time I could handle it.'

He crossed the road and leaned on the railings, the only barrier between land and sea, staring out at the moon path.

She joined him at the railing. 'They all seem to like you in there.'

'I haven't been back there in years. Not since...' He didn't finish the sentence.

'They treated you like a regular.'

'I was once. Place like that, once you're a regular you're always a regular.'

'Sounds nice.' There was a longing in her voice.

'It was. The hotel and the pub belong to the tourists, to the incomers, to people like my parents. Even though I lived at the big house I never ran with the set. The bar belongs to the villagers. When I was home I was in the lifeboat crew. I helped build the jetty.' He nodded over at the wooden structure bobbing about in the gentle waves. 'Euan was with me but there was a difference—no matter how much he rolled up his sleeves and pitched in, he was still the Master, the future Laird. Half those folk in there live in tied cottages. They'd be paying rent to him one day. Now I guess they'll be paying their rent to me.' The prospect was bleak. He didn't want the inevitable separation his title would bring.

'Your father wants you home.' It wasn't a question.

Kit nodded. 'He does and he doesn't. He thinks I should be here learning about the estate but he worries that I'll want to change things. He wants the finance I can bring if I sell my house and bring my investments to the estate but not the power that will give me. He wants a Master of Kilcanon but not me.'

'What happened, Kit? How did Euan die?'

The question was inevitable; they had been approaching this conversation all day. He took a deep, shuddering breath, allowing himself to really confront the past, confront his role in it, for the first time in three long years. 'We were ridiculously competitive. Mum says we would fight over anything and everything. I had to prove I was as good as him despite being younger—despite not being the future Laird. He had to prove his asthma didn't stop him.' Kit gazed out at the bay. He could still see them: two boys night fishing from a dinghy, kayaking over to the nearest island, still visible in the dusky night.

'Anything I could do he had to do better and vice versa, but we were really close even so.' His lips compressed into a hard line. 'We sailed, fished, camped, built dens. It was ridiculously idyllic, looking back. Just look at it, Maddison. Some people hate growing up in a place like this but we thrived. Like some *Boy's Own* adventure. Only it was real life.'

'Sounds amazing.'

'I knew I had no future here and I resented that, I guess. The estate wouldn't support me as well—second sons are useful spares but they can get in the way. So I headed to Cambridge at eighteen, started to build a life away from Kilcanon although I always yearned to come home. We would pick up right where we left off in the holidays, trying to get the better of each other. I just didn't realize that nothing was off limits.'

'Some things should have been.'

Maybe. It was odd now, looking back. Remembering how hurt he had been. The sense of betrayal when Euan had just continued the game that had started before Kit could walk, carried it on to the ultimate conclusion. 'I refused to show Euan how much he had hurt me. I had my pride, after all. I wished he and Eleanor well and I walked away as if I didn't give a damn. I agreed to be best man at their wedding. But it wasn't enough. He wanted my blessing, for me to tell him it was all okay. We were okay.'

'So what did you do?' Maddison placed her soft hand on his; the gleam of victory mixed with whisky gone from her eyes, her pointed chin no longer lifted in triumph, rather her whole body leaned into him in wordless sympathy.

'Do? I refused to give him the satisfaction. I stayed in London, built up my publishing business, dated, came home for holidays and did everything I could to prove that I was better. I was insufferable. Had to coppice the most trees, catch the most fish, build the longest bit of fence, bring home a different girl each time, be the most popular brother with the locals. I was the life and soul of every party. He couldn't compete but it didn't stop him from trying.'

It was easy to look back now and see how angry he had been. Maybe they should have had a good fight and got it out of their systems with some well-aimed punches rather than letting the anger fester for four long years.

'One Christmas we got into a pointless row. We'd often raced across the harbour—row boats, sailing boats, motor boats and, being the insufferable brats we were, kept a running tally. I thought I was ahead, he thought he was and I wouldn't back down. In the end he told me, in the most condescending high-handed way, that if I needed it that much then, okay, we would say it was me.' Kit took another long look at the sea: boyhood playground, beautiful, endless, merciless. 'Of course, I wasn't having that. I insisted we sort the matter out immediately. One last race, winner takes all. He told me not to be stupid and I pushed and pushed until…by then we were both determined to win no matter what the cost. I didn't know how high the cost could be.'

He swallowed, memories washing over him, the spray of salt water on his face, the burning in his arms and legs, the sweet, sweet moment of victory turning sour as he realized something was very wrong.

'His asthma?'

Kit nodded. 'An attack right out there and of course the silly sod had forgotten his inhaler. I went back for him, God, I don't think I've ever rowed as fast in my life, but I wasn't fast enough. I got him to shore, called an ambulance but...I was too late. Too late to save him, too late to forgive him.'

He paused for a long moment. 'This was always the place I longed to be. I was so jealous of Euan, that this was his while I lived in exile.'

'So why haven't you moved back now your parents want you here?'

'How can I? I killed my brother as surely as if I had pushed him off the cliff. I knew his chest was bad that Christmas but I couldn't see beyond my own hurt pride. I forced him to race me and he died. How can I live here? How can

I ever be happy when he's in the ground, knowing I put him there?'

'Oh, Kit.' Her arms were around him, holding him tight, her lips on his cheek, on his jaw, his neck. Her fingers tangled in his hair, her voice enfolding him with whispered comfort. 'You do belong here, Kit, but it's not Euan you have to forgive, it's you. Let it go, Kit. Forgive yourself. Isn't that what Euan would want? Let it go. Live.'

Kit stared out to sea, Maddison's heat, her fire slowly warming him, bringing him painfully back to life. *Isn't that what Euan would want? Was it?* He had no idea.

He put his hands on her shoulders, standing back so he was at arm's length, so that he could see her face, her eyes, her truth. 'Why would you think that?'

'Think what? Think that three years of self-imposed exile, three years of guilt, of estrangement is enough? Because it is, Kit. You didn't kill your brother. He knew the rules, he was an active player, sometimes the instigator, always the main competitor. What happened to him is beyond sadness, beyond grief, but it isn't your fault.'

Kit desperately wished he believed that, but his mind flashed back to that bleak December day. To the pain and anger in his father's eyes, the anguish enfolding his mother, Bridget's sobs and Eleanor's stony-faced grief. The identical looks on their faces when he'd walked wearily into the hospital waiting room. The looks that had told him quite clearly that they knew exactly where the blame lay.

And he had agreed. Had willingly shouldered the toxic burden and let it infect his whole life. He deserved it.

Maddison cupped his cheek, her hand branding him with its gentleness. 'What did Euan want that whole time he was married to Eleanor? For *you* to forgive *him*. He wanted his brother back. What would he say now, if he was here?'

To get over myself. But it wasn't that easy. 'It's not just you that you're hurting.' Her voice was gentle but her words inexorable, beating away at his carefully erected shields. 'Your parents, your sister. They miss you. The way things are they've lost two brothers, two sons. You can't bring Euan back, Kit, but you can give them back you. You can become part of the family again. And sure, it'll hurt. You'll miss him every time you have to make a decision he should have made, perform a task that was his, visit a place he loved, but that way you'll preserve his memory too. Because right now? You're denying him that.'

Kit stared down at her. Was she right? Was his decision to stay away, to keep apart from his family, to carry the burden of Euan's death alone selfish? An excuse to wallow in his grief? Coming home, being part of the family again, moving on would hurt, not with the dull, constant ache he'd carried for the last three years but with sharp, painful clarity, but maybe, just maybe, it was the right thing to do. The right way to honour and remember his brother.

CHAPTER TWELVE

HE HADN'T SLEPT a wink. Kit stared at the window, the first rosy tints of dawn peeking through the flimsy curtains—sunrise came early this time of year. As boys he and Euan would often be up and out, determined to wring every second of adventure out of the long summer days.

Maddison was soft, warm, curled into him like a satisfied kitten, and he shifted, careful not to wake her. She murmured and turned, the sheet slipping to expose the creamy point of her shoulder, red-gold hair tumbling over it like spun sugar. He could nudge her awake, kiss her awake...

Kit slid out of bed and grabbed his clothes. If he woke her then he would make love to her and that, that would be amazing on many levels, especially as it would stop him thinking, stop his brain turning her words over and over and over. But it was time he faced his situation head-on—and he wouldn't be able to do it with a naked Maddison so temptingly within reach.

Everything she had said made sense. He thought that he was truly, fittingly punishing himself by staying away, but all he was doing was running from his troubles. He needed to come home, part of the time at least. He needed to shoulder the responsibilities that were his to bear now that he was Master of Kilcanon. He needed to do more than suggest business ideas to his father; he needed to provide the capital, the manpower and the know-how he could so easily manage. He needed to celebrate his brother's legacy by being part of it, not tarnish it by hiding from it.

Maddison shifted again and the sheet slid a little lower. Kit stopped and stared, his mouth dry as he drank her in. Funny to think he had known her just a few weeks, and that for the beginning of that time he had barely noticed her at all. She looked so different asleep: softer, sweeter, more vulnerable.

But she *was* vulnerable, wasn't she? The realization hit him like a freezing spring wave. That efficient exterior was nothing but a carefully honed act; at heart Maddison Carter was a lost little girl searching for a happily ever after. What had she said she wanted? *Hayrides and clambakes and a huge family Thanksgiving?* He wasn't entirely sure what a clambake was—but he was pretty sure that he wasn't planning to find out.

Kit grimaced, reality stabbing through him along with the dawn sun's rays. *What was he doing?* She worked with him, worked *for* him and he was no Prince Charming. He could offer her a few weeks of fun but he couldn't give her the porch swing, the four children, the clambakes and fireworks. He had his own life to sort out—he didn't know where he would be living, what he would be doing in three *months* let alone three years, thirty years. He didn't think he could promise three months. He didn't know how to.

And Maddison needed security like most people needed air.

Maybe she didn't want security from him. Maybe she was happy with things the way they were but he couldn't risk it. Couldn't risk her getting hurt. Or, a little voice whispered, himself;

he couldn't get too used to having her around. She would be heading away, back to the future she needed, she craved. This thing, whatever it was, had got too deep, too intense far, far too quickly. He curled his hands into fists. There were many difficult decisions he needed to face today but this one was easy. He needed time and space away from Maddison Carter—it was the best thing he could do for her.

Maddison came to with a jolt, aching all over, a sweet, luxurious ache that almost begged her to push harder, again and again. She rolled over, unsure for one moment where she was, why she felt this way: sore, sated, satisfied. The windows were barely covered, the sun shining through the thin filmy curtains. She slumped back onto the soft pillows, the memories running through her mind like a shot-by-shot replay. Sex had never been like that before. Never been so intense, so all-encompassing. She had never been so lost in someone else, so lost to pleasure.

She sat up, her heart thumping.

What had she been thinking? To be so dependent on another person with no guarantees at all that the words, the touches, the intimacy meant anything, would lead anywhere. She had taken her entire rule book and just ripped it up. Maddison curled her hands into tight fists as reality set in, the cold and harsh light of day displacing her sleepy, sated dreams.

Okay, reality check. Last night had been about emotion-driven sex—that was all. That was why it had been so very intense. So all consuming. So very, very good... She was still riding high on adrenaline after her own bout of confessional honesty. It hurt, that opening up, allowing someone in. It hurt to face her own flaws. Sex was some kind of all-purpose plaster, helping make everything feel better, mind, body and soul. And then Kit had trumped her, tearing open his own secrets, facing his own demons.

No wonder their lovemaking had been so hot, both of them trying to lose themselves, forget themselves, seek absolution in the other's touch. But that was all it was. All it could be.

Maddison stretched out an arm and brushed the other side of the bed. It was cold; Kit must have left her some time ago. She pulled her phone off the nightstand. It was still early, not yet seven. He must have left her before dawn. She looked around. No note, no sign of him at all.

A chill brushed her chest and the ache in her limbs intensified, a little less sweet, a little less luxurious. Now the ache just made her wince, a physical reminder of her own vulnerability.

What if he regretted it all? Not just the sex but the emotional honesty? What if he decided their closeness had all been a mistake? There was no way she was going to hand all the power over to him; no way was she going to allow herself to be made vulnerable. She needed to re-erect her barriers and fast.

Maddison showered and dressed quickly, mechanically, building up her armour layer by layer with each brush of her hair, each sweep of the mascara wand, each blotting of her lipstick. Armour was preventative, protective. It kept you strong, kept you alive to fight another day. And the very fact that she felt that she might need it told her everything: she had let Kit in too deeply, too quickly, too intensely. And she didn't trust him not to hurt her.

She didn't trust herself not to let him.

She sank into the easy chair by the bedroom window and stared out at the stunning view, all blues and silvers and greens. It was a living picture, one she could never get tired of as the sky shifted and the sea moved restlessly. In the distance a gannet dropped, a reckless, speedy plunge into the water below, and her stomach dropped with it. She had been that reckless. She had plunged into intimacy with no thought of tomorrow. Would she, like the gannet, resurface with nothing to show for her dive?

She knew better. How many times had her mother told her that *this is the one*? The man who was going to rescue them. The man who was going to give them a home, make them into a real family. Every time Tanya Carter fell all the way in straight away, offering herself up like a sacrifice only to wonder why every time she was left with her heart ripped out, alone and defenceless. Maddison had learned early that you kept your heart locked away, you didn't let anyone into your soul—and you made sure you came out on top, always.

Only where had that knowledge got her? She hadn't allowed Bart into her heart and he had still left her—only for her to crash headlong into an ill-thought-out flirtation. She'd known Kit was dangerous early on but hubristically had thought she was invincible, that she could handle him. And what had happened? She had allowed Kit perilously close. But not all the way in. She wasn't that stupid. Thank goodness.

The ache in her chest intensified. She was so tired of being lonely, that was all. She was ready for her safe, secure happy ever after. No more deviations.

But was she really ready? Maddison sighed, staring blindly out at the sea. These last few weeks had thrown her badly off balance, all her plans, her dreams now up in the air. Did she want to try and get Bart back? She tried to picture the future she had dreamed of but the vision was blurry. No, she wanted more than a loveless marriage of convenience. Did she want to put all her efforts into her career? At least that was going right—but what if she missed out on meeting the right guy? Ended up fifty, alone and childfree?

She wanted it all. Kit's face floated into her mind, that amused smile on his mouth, laughter in the blue eyes. Maddison's mouth twisted. Had she learned nothing? He wasn't even here. Her heart began to beat painfully, each thud reminding her that she was alone once again.

Maybe she needed to look backwards before she looked forwards. Maybe it was time she faced just who she was, who she had been. Maybe that way she would find the answers she needed.

She checked the time again. Seven-thirty. She could do with coffee, juice, something to push away the ache in her head and her chest. What was the etiquette with breakfasting in castles anyway? She doubted that a maid would come in with a breakfast tray. She should find her way to the kitchen and sort out a coffee and a plan. A plan always made everything better.

Resolutely Maddison got to her feet but before she moved a step the door swung open to reveal Kit, fully dressed, shadows emphasizing his eyes, his stubble darker than usual. He looked as if he hadn't slept a wink. Maddison's heart began to beat faster, adrenaline mixing with anticipation and dread. His mouth was set in a grim line, his eyes unsmiling.

'I brought you a coffee.' He held out a huge mug and she took it gratefully, cradling it between her hands, drawing courage from the warmth.

'Thanks, I was about to venture out in search of the kitchen but I didn't have a ball of string long enough to guide me back.' She kept her voice deliberately light and carefree and saw some of the tension leave him. 'It's a beautiful day. Which is a shame because I'd really like to explore the area, I've hardly had a chance to do more than glimpse it, but I really need to be getting back.'

He must know that was a lie. He knew she knew hardly anyone else in London, knew that all her time was spent either working for him, testing out routes with him or on her own with a takeaway. But he didn't challenge her. She hadn't been expecting him to but disappointment stabbed through her anyway. 'I was thinking of staying here a few more days.'

I, not *we*. Not unexpected. 'That's a good idea.'

'I went fishing with my father this morning. There's a lot we need to discuss. About the future of this place. My role in it.'

'Kit,' she said as gently as she could. 'You don't need to explain, not to me.'

He carried on as if she hadn't spoken. 'I feel bad that you have to make your own way back, though. There's a taxi booked to take you all the way to Glasgow and I've bought you a first-class ticket back to London. As a thank you for coming with me.'

'You didn't have to do that.'

'I did.' His mouth tilted. 'You gave up your weekend again. It was very kind of you.'

'Well, thank you.' She took a sip of the scaldingly hot coffee, the pain almost welcome in this falsely polite exchange. 'I meant what I said yesterday, Kit. I'm not Camilla. We didn't make any promises and I'm not the kind of girl who reads wedding bells into every kiss.'

'Not unless you planned it that way.' There was a hint of warmth in his eyes and she wanted to hold on to it, blow it into life, but she held back, wrapping her dignity around her like a protective cloak.

'You know me, always with the plan.' And that, Maddison realized, was the part that was so hard to say goodbye to. He did know her. Almost better than she knew herself. More than anyone else in the whole wide world. And that wasn't enough for him. She wasn't enough.

She'd done good work here. She'd helped him break down some of his guilt, helped ease some of his burden, shown him that he was a man worth knowing. Maybe she'd paved the way for someone with more confidence, someone who didn't care about rejection, someone who knew what they were worth to come in and finish the job. And obviously that thought hurt because she was a little raw right now, but that was a good thing, right? She cared about him; he was her friend and he deserved happiness.

And he had done the same for her. The last couple of weeks she had been *happy*. He'd given her the tools to set her free; she just needed to use them. She was a work in progress, not set in stone after all. The future was hers if she had the courage to embrace it.

'What time is the taxi coming?'

'Soon. It's a couple of hours to Glasgow and a long train ride. I thought you would want to salvage some of your weekend.'

'I'd better pack, then.' She glanced over at the

Halston dress hanging forlornly on the wardrobe door. Last night it had been fantastically, recklessly glamorous. Today it looked limp and a little worse for wear. Like its wearer. 'Don't feel that you have to keep me company, Kit. I have a few things to do and I'd like to make sure I say a proper thank you to your mother before I go. Honestly. I'm fine.'

He paused then nodded, dropping one light kiss onto the top of her head before turning away. It wasn't until Maddison watched Kilcanon disappear behind her that she realized that he hadn't even said goodbye.

Kit swivelled his office chair round and stared unseeingly out across the London skyline. A view that denoted success, status. Just as his expensive chair, his vintage desk, his penthouse office did.

It was cold comfort. In fact there was precious little comfort anywhere. Not here, in this gleaming, glass-clad, supersized office. Not at night in a house far too big for one person, especially a person who barely spent any time there. He'd never noticed before just how bland his house was, like a luxurious and tasteful hotel, not a home. Had he chosen a single one of the varying shades of cream, olive, steel or grey, positioned any one of the statement pieces in the large empty rooms? No, it looked almost exactly the same as it had when the expensive interior decorator had walked away. Like a show home: all facade and no heart.

A bit like his life.

Kit's mouth pressed into a hard line. He knew better than most how hard Maddison's life had been, how she was searching for a place of her own, for security. And what had he done? Made her feel so unwanted that her only option was to leave. Leave a job she loved, a fantastic opportunity she had been headhunted for, in order to avoid him. The irony was that his own notice was in and he would be moving on himself in a couple of months. She should have stayed; he could have moved her to another department if she really wanted to avoid him.

He'd been relieved, that morning in Scotland, at her apparent lack of emotion. Alarm bells should have been screeching. He should have looked deeper but he'd seen what he'd wanted to see. What it was easier for him to see. Again.

He'd told himself that he was doing the right thing, that giving her some space was exactly what they had both needed. But when he'd got back to London she had gone. Family emergency, apparently. Which was interesting because he knew full well that she didn't have any family, not that she was in touch with anyway.

So, it wasn't hard to deduce that she had disappeared in order to avoid seeing him. He should be glad. It made a difficult situation a lot more tenable. No tears and constant phone calls from Maddison; she had more class than that. His mouth thinned. He couldn't just let her vanish into thin air; he should make sure she was okay, that she had somewhere to go. He owed her that. Otherwise he was no better than that idiot on the porch swing.

After all, Bart had obviously had no idea of Maddison's worth, but Kit didn't have that excuse. He knew exactly what she was, *who* she was; he knew just how brightly she shone. Had pushed her away, afraid of being burnt by her flame. The whole time he had been in Scotland he had wished that she were there, had wanted to discuss the compromise he'd made with his father with her. Wanted to hear her thoughts on his plan—a plan that involved spending half the year in Scotland and branching out as a free-lancer again. Using his entrepreneurial skills to help shore up and revitalize the Kilcanon economy.

He'd told himself that pushing her away was for her own good, that she deserved someone better than him but, he realized with scalding shame, he'd been lying to himself all along. He who prided himself on his unflinching honesty. He'd pushed her away because he was scared, because she made him *feel*. She'd made him feel hope. And how had he repaid her? He needed to make sure she was okay. He needed to say sorry. He needed to tell her exactly how brightly she shone.

A call to New York established that Maddison hadn't returned there and that Hope hadn't heard from her. Kit racked his brains. She had never said where she was from. All he knew was that it was a coastal town in New England.

That narrowed it down to thousands of miles of coastline, then.

Kit turned back to his desk and, with a few quick taps, brought Maddison's personnel file up on his screen. He stared at the small yellow envelope. As her line manager he had every right to look in there, more than a right; he had a duty to record appraisals, chart her performance. But, no matter what he told himself, he knew he wasn't looking as a line manager.

He wasn't even looking as a concerned friend.

He missed her. He was pretty damn sure he needed her. Terrifyingly sure that actually he was desperately and irrevocably in love with her.

Love. Was that what this was? This emptiness? This need? This willingness to fall on his sword a thousand times?

He clicked on the icon.

There they were—her application documents, anonymous forms, filled in, filed and forgotten. Until now. He opened her résumé and began reading. She had graduated summa cum laude from Martha George, a small liberal arts college in New York State, and, while there, had spent her summers working as an intern for various

PR agencies before joining a new agency soon after graduating. Two years later she was applying for a job at DL Media.

He scanned further down. Graduated class valedictorian from Bayside High on Cape Cod... Bayside High...*got her.*

But he needed more. He couldn't just turn up in a strange town armed with a photo of her and track her down, could he? He closed the document, opening up her employee details instead. Name, address, Social Security number...there it was. Next of Kin. Only it was blank. She had cut her mother completely out of her life.

What must that be like? His own parents were still hurting, still recovering from Euan's death, from Kit's own emotional and physical distance, but they were there, always there. What must it be like having nobody at all to rely on?

Kit opened another couple of documents at random: appraisals, the move from PR to editorial, her references. It was all in order and yet it told him nothing. Finally he clicked on the last document, her college reference. It was a breakdown of her entire time there, classes taken, grades achieved—and her scholarship recommendation.

He read through the recommendation, words jumping out.

Despite her difficult background...
Three jobs...
Tenacious and hardworking...
Ambitious...
Legal emancipation...
Needs a chance...
No parental support, emotionally or financially...

Seeing her past written there so baldly hit him in a way her confession hadn't. No wonder she pushed everyone away. No wonder she always had to be in control, couldn't show that she needed anyone.

She had never been able to rely on anyone.

Well, hard luck. He was going to be there for her whether she wanted him to be or not. And when he knew she was okay, then he would walk away. If that was what she truly wanted. Only if that was what she truly wanted.

He'd thought that keeping the rest of the world

at bay was what he'd deserved, that he owed Euan a lifetime of remorse and loneliness. Wouldn't it be better to honour his brother's legacy by living? By feeling? The good *and* the bad.

Kit walked back to his desk and read the reference again, noting down the address.

He was going to find out exactly what made Maddison Carter tick, and when he had done so he was going to fix her. He was going to make everything better for someone else for once in his life, no matter what it cost him.

CHAPTER THIRTEEN

MADDISON'S HANDS GREW clammy and she gripped the steering wheel so tight the plastic bit into her palms. Ahead of her the road segued smoothly onto the bridge that separated Cape Cod from the mainland.

The bridge that would take her home.

It was eight years since she had bid it farewell in her rear-view mirror. Waved and sworn never to return. Up until today she had kept that vow.

But it was time to face her demons, confront her past—then maybe she could move forward. Maybe she too would finally deserve some kind of happiness. Her stomach twisted and she gulped in air against the rising panic. Would she be able to find happiness without Kit?

No. This wasn't about Kit. This was about her, Maddison, finally taking stock of who she was and where she had come from. This was about moving on. This was about learning to be happy. If she could…

The bridge soared over the narrow strip of water separating the Cape from the mainland. Mouth set, eyes straight ahead, Maddison maintained a steady speed over the bridge and onto the highway, which ran the full length of the Cape all the way up to Provincetown on the very tip. She wound down her window and the smell hit instantly: salt and gorse. Despite everything she breathed in deeply, letting the familiar air fill her lungs. Despite everything it whispered to her that she was home.

Her turn-off was thirty miles up the Cape, at the spot where the land narrowed and twisted, like an arm raised in victory. She turned instinctively, driving on autopilot, until she found herself entering the small town of Bayside.

Bayside always looked at its best in early summer, when everything was spruced up ready for the seasonal influx that quadrupled the town's population. The freshly painted shopfronts gleamed in the morning sun, the town had an air of suppressed anticipation just as it did every

May, a stark contrast to the weary fade of September.

But some things had changed; several cycle-hire stores had sprung up offering helmets, kiddie trailers and tandems as well as a bewildering assortment of road and trail bikes. Maddison's mouth twisted as she remembered how she had been teased for riding her rusty bike around the town, not driving like her classmates. She guessed she had just been ahead of the curve. The cycle shops weren't the only new stores; driving slowly, Maddison noticed an assortment of new delis, coffee shops, organic cafes and bakeries, many of which wouldn't have been out of place in the Upper East Side or on Stoke Newington Church Street. It was a long way away from the ice-cream parlours and burger joints of her youth.

Bayside had always been a town divided, not once, but two or three times. Locals versus visitors. Summer-home owners versus two-week vacationers. Vacationers versus day trippers. And at the bottom of the heap, divided from everyone, were the town's poor, dotted here and there in trailers or falling-down cottages, on scrubland worth millions less than the prime real estate on the ocean edge. That had been Maddison's world.

Her stomach tightened as she drove out of town, past the small, dusty road that led to Bill's Bar, a small, shabby establishment frequented only by locals—her mother's second home. If she took that road and pulled in would she see the all-too-familiar sight of her mother, propping up the bar, another drink in front of her? She accelerated past, heading for the Bayside Inn where she had reserved a room. Once she'd asked them for a job and been turned away. Now her money was as good as anyone's.

Two hours later, showered and refuelled by some excellent coffee, Maddison was back in the car, continuing on the road out of town following the shore. The town was situated by a huge natural bay and the beaches were sheltered, the water warm and safe; in low tide it was possible to walk out for what seemed like miles and still only be waist deep. The beautiful sand-dune beaches on the other side of town plunged swimmers straight into the icy swell of the ocean, where seals frolicked within swimming distance—and where the seals swam the great whites weren't far behind. Property overlooking the ocean on both sides was at a premium and Maddison drove past tall electronic gates prohibiting access to the vast, sprawling houses within, their views worth more than their opulent interiors.

Maddison pulled into the ungated driveway of one of the oldest and more modest houses: a two-storey white-shingled house. True, anywhere else the five-bedroomed dwelling with its beautiful wraparound porch, outside pool and beach views from every room would be pretty impressive, but it lacked the helipad and pool houses of some of its more vulgar neighbours. On one side stood a separate double garage, and Maddison looked up at the apartment overhead, that sense of coming home intensifying. This was the first place where she had ever had the luxury of security.

She rang the bell and waited, wiping her hands on her skirt, trying not to jiggle impatiently. No answer. Maddison looked around, hope draining away. Why hadn't she called ahead? The house might have changed hands, or the own-

ers be away. This whole impetuous road trip
was probably a waste of time, a self-indulgent
wallow in memory lane. She took a step back,
poised to turn away, but the movement was ar-
rested by the sound of a key turning. Maddison
turned, hope hammering in her chest, the relief almost too much when the door opened to
reveal a familiar face. Mrs Stanmeyer. A little
older, but her blonde hair was still swept back in
an elegant coil, she was still as regally straight-
backed, exquisitely dressed in linen trousers and
a white silk shirt.

'Hello, can I help…?' The voice trailed off.
'Maddison? Maddison Carter? Oh, my dear girl.'

As Mrs Stanmeyer's face relaxed into a welcoming smile and she stepped forward, arms
outstretched to pull Maddison into a hug, the
pain in Maddison's chest, the load she had carried since she was eighteen, the load that had
seemed unbearable since she left Scotland, less-
ened just a little. Enough to make it manageable.

'Maddison, oh, my dear, come on in. I am so
very glad to see you.'

Maddison found herself ushered into the wide,
spacious hallway. Little had changed, she was

relieved to see, the house still a tasteful blend of creams and blues, beautiful but practical in a home where children ran straight in from the beach and most of the day was spent outside. Mrs Stanmeyer led her through the living/dining/family room that made up most of the first floor and out onto the deck where a trio of cosy wooden love seats were pulled up invitingly.

'It's so lovely to see you,' Mrs Stanmeyer said as they settled themselves onto the seats, iced water flavoured with fresh lemons on the table before them. 'I have often wondered how you were.'

For the first time in eight years guilt hit Maddison. How could she have cut everyone off so completely when some people had done nothing but offer her help and support?

'This is the first time I've come back,' she admitted, her eyes fixed on the sand dunes and the gleam of blue sea beyond. 'I'm sorry. Sorry I didn't call or email you, sorry I didn't try. I just wanted to wipe it all out. Start again.'

'And how has that gone for you?'

'I thought it was going perfectly. I thought I had reinvented myself, that I was untouchable.'

She grimaced. 'But I guess I never stopped judging myself. In the end I was the one still looking down on me, never believing I was worthy of anything, deserved anything. Maybe that's why I spent the last few years chasing after all the wrong things.' She swallowed hard, the lump in her throat making words almost impossible. 'And now it's too late. I'm worried that it's too late.' Her mouth quivered and she covered it with one hand.

'Oh, Maddison. It's never too late. The girl I knew, the girl with three jobs when she was just fourteen? The girl who supported herself at sixteen and still graduated as class valedictorian, she knew that.'

Maddison looked up at that. Was that how Mrs Stanmeyer saw her? Not as a monumental mess but as a survivor? 'Supported myself and graduated thanks to you. If you hadn't given me a job when no one else would, offered me the maid's room, sorted out the scholarship to Martha George, I don't know where I would have ended up.'

The older woman reached out and laid a hand on Maddison's arm. 'I didn't do anything, Maddison. If anything I felt guilty for not doing more—a child of your age here all winter on her own, cleaning for me! But you were so determined and so proud, I knew you wouldn't take charity. As for the scholarship, all I did was recommend you. You did the rest yourself.'

For the first time in maybe forever a glow of achievement warmed her. She *had* worked hard, saved hard, studied hard. Hadn't allowed her beginnings to define her end. But she knew that without the home, the money, the trust Mrs Stanmeyer had shown her it would have been a far harder journey.

'I wondered...' Maddison twisted her hands together, trying to find the right words. 'I wondered why you helped me, if maybe it was... if I was...' She glanced through the open glass doors to the large sideboard, at the collection of family portraits gathered there. She had dusted each of them time and time again, searching for some kind of resemblance between herself and the two blonde, elegant daughters and the boyish, handsome son. There were more photos now, babies and small, round children playing in the sand. 'Did you help me because your son... Is he my father?'

The smile faded from Mrs Stanmeyer's face, replaced by a weary sadness. 'Oh, Maddison. If you were my granddaughter I hope I'd have done better than employing you as my maid and housing you in a room over the garage. I don't think Frank even knew your mother. He was away interning the summer you were conceived.'

Warring emotions hit her, intense disappointment that she could never be part of this family mingled with relief that she wasn't the guilty secret hidden away in the maid's room after all. 'Do you know who it was? Who my father is?'

Mrs Stanmeyer shook her head. 'No, but I knew your mother. You look very much like her, you know, the same hair, the same eyes—and the same ambition. I'd known your grandmother a very long time but I really got to know Tanya the summer before you were born. She was hoping for a scholarship to Martha George too, and I was already on the admissions board.'

Maddison stared. Her mother had applied to the elite liberal arts college? She didn't remember her even opening a book, let alone studying. At least she certainly hadn't after Grandma died.

'My mom?' Her voice squeaked despite herself and she stopped, silent. She wasn't supposed to care.

Mrs Stanmeyer nodded. 'It was a scandal when she fell pregnant with you. Everyone said it was such a waste of potential. I think some thought it a judgement—she was just so alive, so free, so sure she could do it all. She told me she didn't care what they said, that she was excited about the future, that she would raise you and study at night. Like you she was very independent. She moved out of your grandmother's house into the trailer when you were still a baby, determined not to ask for help. I think they clashed a lot.'

'They did, but they loved each other too,' Maddison admitted. 'She was devastated when Grandma died.' She took a sip of the ice-cold water, trying to reconcile this picture of a vibrant, ambitious teen mom with the bitter reality. 'What happened? Because the woman I knew? She had no ambition beyond the next drink, the next boyfriend.'

Mrs Stanmeyer shook her head. 'I wish I knew.

I saw a little of her when you were a baby and a toddler and everything seemed fine. I was a friend of your grandmother's, you see, since we were girls ourselves, and I always took an interest in your mother. I knew she found it hard, making enough money, keeping up her studies and raising you, but she was very optimistic. Your grandmother's illness hit her hard but at that time my own girls were growing up, had their own teen worries and troubles and I didn't see your mother—or you—for several years. I heard gossip, of course, but I discounted it as mutterings of scandal-loving old cats. Maybe I shouldn't have been so quick to judge them. When I next saw her it was as if something had broken inside her. She seemed to have given up. I tried to help but she pushed me away, many times.'

Maddison's eyes burned and the pressure in her chest swelled to almost unbearable degrees. It had been so long since she had thought of her mother without scorn and anger but she could all too vividly imagine the struggling young woman, breaking down under the burden of poverty and hardship. And sitting here contemplating a bleak future of her own making, a future without Kit, she understood, a little, the intoxicating appeal of just checking out of life.

Maybe her bleakness showed on her face because Mrs Stanmeyer's voice was very gentle, very kind. 'What's brought you home, Maddison, after all this time?'

She blinked, trying in vain to hold back the tears that had been building but not allowed to fall since the moment she had driven away from Kilcanon, each one scalding her as it escaped. 'I thought I had it all planned out but I'm lost. And I have no idea how to find my way.'

'Do you have any plans for today, dear?' Mrs Stanmeyer—Lydia, as she had instructed Maddison to call her—put a plate of pancakes, bacon and maple syrup in front of Maddison as she spoke. 'Eat up. You are far too thin.'

In some ways the last twenty-four hours had been like stepping into a much-loved and cherished daydream. Mrs Stanmeyer had insisted she cancel her room at the inn and stay with her, putting Maddison in the whitewashed corner room with views out over the ocean on two sides. When Maddison had been the live-in maid she had always pretended that the room was hers. It wasn't the largest or the fanciest, but the views were superb and the sloping ceiling gave it a quaint, old-fashioned air.

'Thank you.' Maddison picked up her fork, not needing much more encouragement to get stuck in. Maybe it was the sea air, maybe the best night's sleep she had had in years, but she had woken with a hearty appetite. 'This looks amazing but you really shouldn't have gone to so much trouble.' Maybe not, but seeing as she *had*… Maddison speared a piece of bacon and pancake, dousing them liberally in the amber syrup, before allowing herself to savour the taste. 'I need to get in touch with the office and take some leave officially. I just kind of left…'

Did she even have a job anymore? After all, she was technically absent without leave; she doubted she could claim compassionate leave for an imaginary family crisis. How could she, organized, always-planning-ahead Maddison, have just walked out on her job—would there even be a place for her in New York? Maddison shivered, cold despite the sun on her shoulders.

She had thrown everything away in her impetuous flight.

The doorbell rang and Maddison pushed her chair back, automatically readying herself to answer it. 'Don't be silly, dear. You eat.' Lydia gave her a gentle push back into her seat as she walked past her and into the hallway.

Maddison scooped some more food onto her fork but didn't move it off her plate, her mind whirring. She would do what she had to here and then what? Sort out her job situation. Contact Kit.

Should she have left Kit without telling him how she felt?

How could she have told him when she'd barely admitted it to herself?

'Maddison.' She looked up as Lydia called her. There was a curious tone in her voice, curiosity mixed with satisfaction. 'It's for you.'

For her? Who on earth could be visiting her? Maybe someone at the inn had mentioned seeing her, maybe an old school friend had heard that she was back—but no, she hadn't been much of one for friends. Her high-school boyfriend had married in his early twenties, but even if he hadn't she couldn't imagine he'd cared enough about her to hotfoot it over the second she sailed back into town.

Her stomach shifted and she clasped one hand to it. Surely not her mother...

Maddison got to her feet, reaching out to the table for support, and moved slowly into the hallway and blinked, trying to focus on the tall, dishevelled man standing there. 'Kit?' She wasn't sure if she thought it, breathed it or shouted his name aloud. 'What are you doing here? You look tired,' she added as he came into focus. His skin was almost grey, his eyes bloodshot and his chin darker than usual with extra stubble.

'Isn't that the point of a red eye? I left London yesterday afternoon, spent several hours in Toronto and landed in Boston...' he checked his watch, swaying a little as he did so '...about three hours ago.'

He sounded so matter-of-fact. As if his turning up here were completely normal. She blinked. 'But why?'

'If I were you, Maddison, I would take poor Mr Buchanan into the kitchen and feed him coffee and pancakes before you interrogate him any further. I am heading out for the day so please both make yourselves at home. There are spare bathing suits and towels in the drying room if you want to go to the beach. Help yourself to anything you need.'

Before Maddison could say anything Lydia had whisked out of the door, leaving them quite alone. She stood still, staring at Kit. She wanted to touch him, check she wasn't imagining things, but she didn't quite dare.

'Was that coffee I heard mentioned?' Kit asked hopefully. 'I drank at least a gallon in Boston before collecting the hire car but I think it wore off somewhere around Plymouth.'

'Coffee? Yes, come on in.' It *must* be a dream, Maddison decided as she led him through into the kitchen. In which case she was going with it; she hadn't had a dream this comforting in, well, in forever.

There was still a stack of pancakes in the warmer and some bacon in the pan and she ladled a substantial helping of both onto a plate, handing them and a large mug of coffee to Kit.

He received them rapturously, almost inhaling the first cup of coffee and half the plate of food before leaning back with a satisfied stretch. 'These are good. I couldn't get a first-class flight or a direct flight so I have suffered more hours than I care to admit of limited leg room and plastic food. But for these pancakes I would fly all the way to Australia.'

'But you didn't fly all this way for pancakes.' Maddison pushed her plate away; even Kit's hearty enjoyment of his breakfast hadn't rekindled her appetite.

'No.'

'How did you find me?'

'It's a good thing I like treasure hunts. You've covered your tracks pretty well. Actually,' he confessed, pouring a second large cup of coffee, 'I didn't. Expect to find you here, that is. This address was my first—and only—clue.'

Maddison cast around for the words that would somehow make it all right. The words that would make her worthy of a man who had flown across the world to find her with nothing but an old address to spark the hunt. She didn't have them.

'Why?'

'I wanted to make sure you're all right.'

She stared at him incredulously. 'You wanted

to make sure I was all right? So you flew to Toronto and then to Boston and then drove here just to check up on me?'

'That about sums it up,' he agreed. 'I was worried about you. I didn't handle Scotland very well.' His eyes gleamed with warmth and something deeper, something she hadn't seen in them before and yet recognized instantly.

Maddison was suddenly, unaccountably shy. She didn't know if she could handle whatever he'd come here to say, not yet. Not until she'd done what she'd come here to do. 'How tired are you?'

'I don't know. Part of me is so wired on caffeine and sunshine I could run a marathon, the other part exhausted enough to sleep for the proverbial hundred years. Why?'

'I wondered if you wanted to go on a treasure hunt. With me.'

Kit smiled then, a slow, sweet smile that wiped the weariness off his face, and Maddison's heart leapt as she watched his eyes spark back to life. 'A treasure hunt? What's the prize?'

She wanted to answer *me* but how could she presume he wanted her, would think her any kind of prize? Sure, he had flown here but he hadn't told her why, had made no move towards her, uttered no words of love. It might have been pique or anger that had set him off to hunt her down.

'I'm not sure,' she said instead. 'But we'll know it when we find it.'

CHAPTER FOURTEEN

SHE LOOKED VULNERABLE: too thin, too pale, all the vitality leached out of her, and all Kit wanted to do was hold her close and tell her that it didn't matter, none of it mattered. But he couldn't, not yet. Because to her it did. And that meant it mattered to him too. Whatever Maddison had returned home to do, he would support her with, help her with.

Maddison drove, pointing out that he hadn't slept in goodness knew how many hours and was liable to find himself on the wrong side of the road even if he didn't doze off, and Kit didn't argue, happy to sit relaxed in the passenger seat, enjoying the view. Maddison's home town was picture-perfect, all blue skies, beaches and quirky, local shops all located in painted, wood-shingled buildings. It was like a film set.

'So, what are we looking for?' he asked at last as she turned into a small housing development.

Cheerful detached houses sat on hilly lots, each garden flowing into the next, trees all around them. He could imagine children biking up the driveways, playing ball by the hoops fastened in many of the garage roofs.

She didn't answer for a long moment, pulling up outside a corner house. It was a pretty blue wooden house, a covered porch on one side. Maddison stared at it, her heart in her eyes. 'Me,' she said finally. 'We're looking for me. I want to see where it all went wrong, where I went wrong.'

He wanted to contradict her, tell her that she didn't have a wrong bone in her body, but he sensed this wasn't what she needed, not today, and instead just nodded. He'd guessed as much. 'Okay. Is this where we start?'

'This was my grandma's house.' She killed the engine and shifted to face him, her eyes very green in her pale face. 'My mom was very young when she had me and I didn't know my dad. When I was little she worked a lot so I came here. My grandma told me that she wished I could live there forever and I wished it too, that I could spend every night in my little yellow bedroom with the rocking horse. But my mom wanted to prove she could do it on her own and so most evenings she'd pick me up and take me home. Then, when I was seven, I got my wish. We moved in. Only my grandma was really sick.' Her mouth quivered.

Kit wanted to pull her in tight and tell her everything was okay. But it wasn't, not yet. Not until she had told him, whatever she needed to. 'Then what happened?'

Maddison stared at the house, her eyes unfocused as if she could see her younger self playing in the wooded yard. 'Then she died. My mom was supposed to inherit the house, only there were medical bills and she had to sell it. I think that's when it all got too much for her.'

'How about you? How did it affect you?'

She didn't answer for a long moment, her hands twisting in her lap, then turned back to the wheel and restarted the engine. It wasn't until she was backing out of the driveway that she answered, her voice hoarse with repressed tears. 'Like I'd lost my world. I guess I had.'

It took nearly a quarter of an hour to reach her next destination. Maddison headed out of town before taking an abrupt turn down an untreated road, the woods encroaching on both sides of the rough track. At various intervals the trees were hacked back and small cottages or trailers built in the scrubby wastelands. Kit held on as the car bumped over stones and potholes. 'I hope you got a good insurance deal,' he said through gritted teeth.

Maddison didn't answer, her focus on the road ahead. Finally, just when Kit was sure his insides had been turned into a cocktail definitely shaken not stirred, she pulled into a rough clearing. At the back, on breeze blocks, stood a trailer, the windows boarded up and the door swinging off its hinges. Surely not…

Kit stared at the trailer, unable to disguise his revulsion. 'Please tell me this is where you lost your virginity or went all Blair Witch,' he said. 'Please don't tell me you lived here.' But she was afraid of the dark. She'd mentioned being hungry and cold. He'd known it was bad. He just had hoped it wasn't this bad.

'It was only meant to be temporary. Till Mom got some money and a proper job.' Her voice cracked. 'We had a fund, the Maddison and

Mom fund, and we were going to use it to travel, to get a proper house, to go to Disneyland. But it was hard to save even before Grandma died and afterwards…I'd get ill or needed new shoes or there were bills and so the fund kept getting depleted even though Mom worked all the time.'

'Who looked after you while she worked?' But he already knew the answer. 'You were a child. Alone, out here?'

'She said I was never to tell. That if they knew they'd take me away.'

Kit thought back to his own wild childhood. Roaming free, swimming, sailing, hiking, utterly secure in his parents' love. He'd never realized just how lucky he had been. How lucky he still was in many ways. How much he had taken for granted, how much he had pushed away.

Maddison carried on, her voice expressionless, as if she were reading from a script. 'She got more and more tired and then she was just angry all the time. One night she picked up the phone to call for pizza and the phone had been cut off. She was so mad, swearing and screaming and kicking things—and then she left. Picked up her car keys and walked away. I thought she'd gone for pizza but she didn't come back and when I woke in the morning she was passed out on the sofa. She'd never really drunk before that but I think she just needed to stop thinking—and the drink helped her forget for a time at least.'

It didn't take too much detective work to guess the rest. 'And she carried on drinking?'

Maddison nodded. 'Soon I became that child, you know, the one no one wants to sit next to in case they catch something. It's hard to keep clean when the hot water is cut off and you don't have a washing machine. It's hard to look smart when all your clothes are second-hand.' Her voice dripped with bitterness and Kit's heart ached to hear it. Ached for the lonely, neglected child.

'And no one did anything? Your teachers? Social workers?'

'A few tried to talk to me but I said I was fine. I didn't want to be taken away. This might not look like much but it was all I knew. Mom made just enough of an effort when she had to come in to school, at least she did back then. I'm glad she's not still here,' she said, her voice shaking. 'I'm glad she got out.'

The trailer looked like no one had lived there for a very long time and Kit was relieved when Maddison reversed and pulled away. He wasn't sure he could have looked inside the trailer and not cracked. 'Do you know where she is?'

'Mrs Stanmeyer said she got clean the year I left. Apparently she finally got her degree and got a job as a teacher, can you believe it? Married three years ago and moved to Chatham. She has a little girl, she's about two. My sister.'

'Are you going to go and see her?'

Maddison's mouth trembled. 'I haven't decided.'

'I'll come with you, if you want me to.'

'Thank you. Not today. I'm not ready. But maybe tomorrow.'

She was talking about tomorrow. With him. Kit waited for panic to hit him but it was gone as if it had never been. Tomorrow was just a word.

'Okay, in that case, where next?'

'Next?' Her mouth curved into an unexpected smile. 'Clue Three. The reinvention of Maddison Carter.'

She took them back into town, driving straight through the centre and turning into a large car

park situated beside playing fields and an offi-
cial-looking building that proclaimed itself 'Bayside High, Home of the Sea Hawks.'

'Sea Hawks, huh?' Kit tried to lighten the
mood. 'Were you a cheerleader? I bet you looked
amazing in one of those skirts.'

'No, girls like me didn't get to be cheerlead-
ers. Although you're right, I would have looked
pretty darn good in that skirt.'

'So which were you? The jock, the princess.
The geek? Ally Sheedy?'

He was relieved to hear her choke out a laugh.
'Which do you think? I was Ally Sheedy both
before and after the makeover. Only mine was
better. A real reinvention.'

'I'm glad to hear it.'

'In junior high I began working. I was too
young for a proper job so I hustled for work:
babysitting, car washing, grocery shopping, anything I could do to get money so I could dress
better, get a bike, try and fit in. By the time I
reached high school I knew I needed more. I
needed to take control of my life so I took on as
much work as I could get, studied like mad and

started to plan my exit route. I moved out the day I turned sixteen and became a live-in maid at Mrs Stanmeyer's.'

'At sixteen? Was that even legal?'

Maddison nodded. 'She hated that I insisted on working. She would have let me have a room for free, helped me out with money for much less work, but I refused any sign of charity—I'd been the town's trash for long enough. I wanted to earn every cent, make sure everyone knew I wasn't like my mother. I loved living there. I had the room over the garage. It was the first time I'd felt safe in a really long time.' There was a wealth of untold detail in that last statement and Kit curled his hands into fists, hating how it was too late to make any of it all right.

'I just wanted to fit in,' she almost whispered. 'I wanted to be one of the cool kids, the ones who were so secure they knew exactly who they were and what they deserved.'

'That's understandable.'

'It was no use trying with the girls, my social status was too low. So I targeted the boys. Targeted one boy. It was almost too easy. I could afford to dress better, get my hair cut and I knew boys liked to look at me. The next step was finding out what else he liked and making sure I liked it too, that we met at the same movies, in the same comic-book store, that we always had something to talk about. No one could believe it, Jim Squires, captain of the football team, and Maddison Carter. But when he held my hand in the hallway or I wore his varsity jacket I knew I belonged. At last. I was safe.

'That's when I knew what I wanted. I wanted to leave this Maddison behind and become someone else, the kind of girl who expected to walk down a hallway holding the hottest boy in school's hand, the kind of girl that took dates and friends and proms and an allowance for granted. The kind of girl who had never worked one job, let alone three, who had never set foot inside a trailer. And so when I left here I made it up, invented the life I wished I had. I think at times I even believed my own lies, I've been living them so long. I'm pathetic.'

'Pathetic?' Kit stared at her, incredulous. Was that really what she thought? What she believed? 'You had nothing and you didn't let it stop you. You worked your socks off to achieve your dream. I admire you, Maddison. You're the strongest, bravest person I know. You are absolutely incredible.'

The words reverberated round and round her head, his eyes shining with sincerity and truth. Maddison wanted to believe him but she couldn't, not yet. She pulled away, driving away from the school, away from her memories, away from his words.

Maddison didn't stop until she reached the car park by her favourite beach. She parked haphazardly and jumped out, the sun's warmth a shock after the air-conditioned car. Kit stepped warily out of the car but she didn't acknowledge him, instead turning and walking across the car park, along the boardwalk and past the clam shack until she reached the beach. The smell of fried clams hit her, mingled with the salt in the sea air. The scent of a dozen beach parties.

Despite the heat of the day it was quiet, just a few pre-school families about—the schools not due to break up for another couple of weeks. Maddison pulled her shoes off and walked, barefoot, through the foot of the dunes, wincing as her feet struck the heated sand. Kit matched her step for step, not saying a word, allowing her to set the pace.

'I had this fantasy that my dad was one of the summer-home owners. That his parents hadn't let him acknowledge me but that one day he would stride into school and scoop me up and take me away to live that gilded life. They'd come to town, the summer kids, with their platinum credit cards and their boats and their country-club memberships, and I wanted to be one of them so much it actually hurt, right here.' She tapped her chest.

'Once I got to high school I knew that my daddy wasn't coming for me, that he probably didn't even know I existed. But I still wanted that life. When I moved to New York it was with one goal: to find the right man who could give me the right kind of life and marry him.'

Kit nodded. 'All you wanted was a family. You told me that almost straight away. Four children who would have the most perfect childhood ever. I don't think that's such a terrible crime, Maddison. If you wanted to marry for status or jewels or a platinum credit card of your own, then that would be understandable, considering what you've been through, but you didn't. You wanted a family. A family you could keep safe.'

'And then I started to spend time with you.' She stopped and swallowed, trying to find the right words. 'It had all gone wrong. I thought I knew exactly what I was doing, had found the right guy, but Bart derailed all my plans and knocked my confidence. I arrived in the UK knowing I had to start all over again. When you suggested I spend my weekends doing the treasure trails with you I agreed mainly because I thought it might make Bart jealous, but soon it was more. A lot more. I liked your company. I liked you. And I thought, why not? I was only in the UK for a short while, why not have some fun? Deviate from the grand plan just for a while. I didn't expect to fall in love with you.'

Her words hung there as she kept walking, afraid that if she stopped or turned back then he would walk away. Would leave her. 'But I did. I did fall in love with you. Me, Maddison Carter with my plans and my dreams and my whole *love is for losers* mindset. Guess I wasn't as good at the game as I thought, huh? The ironic thing was that if you had been anyone else it would have been fine, but how could I tell you the truth when you were so adamant that love wasn't for you? How could I open up when you have the kind of background I've been searching for? What could I say? "Please, Kit, I used to want to marry someone rich and important but that's not why I've fallen for you." I wish you weren't. I wish you didn't have any of it. I don't want you to think I played you. Because when I was with you I wasn't playing at all.'

She hadn't planned on telling him any of this, but once the words had spilled out she realized that she was free. Free of her past, her secrets, her schemes, her plans. She had no idea what happened next but that was okay. And if Kit turned, left and she never saw him again, then that was okay as well because she had given it her best shot. A real shot, not a fake, perfectly thought-out, planned response.

She'd given him her heart.

Maddison turned, drinking him in. The faint sea breeze ruffled his hair as he stood at the foot of the sand dunes, his eyes fixed on the endless ocean. 'Why did you come here, Kit?'

'To find you,' he said simply. 'I left Scotland full of plans and the one person I wanted to share them with wasn't there, had just disappeared. I didn't think you were a quitter, Maddison, in fact I knew you weren't, so for you to just up and disappear? Whatever was going on it seemed to me you needed my help. I wanted to help.'

He passed a hand through his hair, rumpling it into an even more disordered state. 'I was a mess that morning in Scotland. Everything had changed in twenty-four hours. Thanks to you I could confront my feelings about Euan, admit it wasn't just guilt I felt but anger—anger at him for dying, for competing, for not fighting hard enough that night. Anger at myself for pushing him. For holding on to my bitterness when I had long since fallen out of love with Eleanor. Thanks to you I really spoke to my dad, about that night, about the future.'

'Sounds intense.'

'Oh, it was quite the fishing session. And then there was you. In my bed. Making me feel things I still wasn't ready to face—that I had been in no way the kind of man that deserved a girl like you. It seemed easier to just let you go but as soon as you were gone I realized I wanted to fix everything, fix me, make myself worthy of you.'

He stepped close and took her hand. 'I missed you, Maddison. I missed you planning every little detail, I missed you searching out every clue, I missed you finishing my crossword, I even missed that damn list. I missed the way you challenge me.' His eyes dropped to her mouth. 'You only spent two nights in my bed but I haven't slept right since. My dreams are full of you, Maddison Carter.'

'I had to come back here,' Maddison said, needing him to understand. 'I needed to face who I was, who I am now. But all I see is that if you're not with me then my life is empty, even with all the security in the world. You flew across the world for me.' Her mouth wobbled. 'I don't deserve that.'

Kit raised one of her hands to his lips and her heart leapt at the old-fashioned gesture. 'You do. You deserve it all. All the security your heart desires.' He smiled down at her. 'Four children, the house, anything you need.'

'Your family needs you, Kit. Your father needs you even if he won't say so.'

'I know and I have obligations in Kilcanon that I've ignored for long enough. I hope you would be happy to spend some of the year there, but we wouldn't have to live in Scotland all the time. We could have a place in London or a house here on the Cape, whatever you wanted.' His mouth twisted into a smile. 'Fourth of July, clambakes, hayrides, Thanksgiving—I'm willing to give it all a try.'

The last clamp finally loosened from her heart. 'I think as long as we're together I have everything I need.'

'So you're saying yes?'

'To what?' But she knew; it was in the blazing blue of his eyes, the curve of his mouth, the heat in his hands.

'To me, to us, to forever.'

Maddison finally allowed herself to reach up, to pull his head down to hers, to press her mouth to his. It was like coming home at long, long last. 'Yes,' she breathed against the warmth of his lips. 'I'm saying yes. To forever.'

EPILOGUE

One year later

KIT SHIFTED FROM foot to foot, anxiously scanning the rows of chairs, looking beyond the seated people to the sun-filled horizon beyond. *Where is she?* He took a deep breath. He should be calmer; after all, they *were* actually already married. Maddison had been very keen to marry him in his kilt but had reluctantly conceded that the Cape Cod beach in summer wasn't the most appropriate place for thickly woven wool and a formal tux—and Kit hadn't wanted to wait a full year before claiming his bride. The answer was a happy compromise—two weddings. A small, private spring service in Kilcanon church and now, two months later, a blessing and party on the Cape.

He scanned the rows of people, all decked out in their summer best: his parents and Bridget were in the front row, looking relaxed and happy after a couple of weeks of sun and playing tourist. His father seemed years younger—handing some of the business responsibilities over to Kit had obviously relieved him of a great burden. They still clashed—they wouldn't be Buchanans if they didn't—but his father grudgingly admitted that some of Kit's ideas weren't too crazy and had thrown himself into setting up the new distillery with enthusiasm. Bridget had finished university this month and had asked Kit if there was a place for her on the family estate, an offer he had accepted straight away. Bridget's presence would make it easier for Maddison and him to spend the summers and long vacations here on the Cape, just as he had promised her they would.

Next to the Buchanans sat a beaming Mrs Stanmeyer clutching a hanky just in case—she had cried throughout the first wedding and had declared her intention to do exactly the same this time round. Further back Kit noticed Hope, his old assistant, clutching the hand of a handsome dark-haired man, a soft smile on her face.

In the back row a beautiful woman in her early

forties sat tensely on the aisle seat, her hands locked, her face set. Maddison still didn't have an easy relationship with her mother, their interactions were very formal and stilted, but they were both trying. But he knew that Maddison adored being a big sister, having blood kin of her own. And, stilted or not, Maddison had hosted Thanksgiving in the house they had bought on the Cape with her family, old and new, around her.

And at that moment the aria she loved so much began to swell out all around them, the guests got to their feet and Kit turned, met a pair of sparkling green eyes and was lost once again.

Maddison hadn't wanted to be given away—after all, she didn't have anyone to ask—so instead of leaning on someone else's arm she was clasping a small hand. It might not be customary for the bride and her flower girl to walk down the aisle hand in hand but Savannah wasn't just a flower girl, she was her little sister. She was hope. Testament that people could change, that the future was unwritten.

The small hand tugged at hers and Maddison bent down.

'Kit looks really handsome,' her small sister whispered and Maddison dropped a kiss on the fair curls, careful not to disturb the carefully arranged flowers. 'I know,' she whispered back.

He didn't look as formally handsome as he had in Kilcanon, clad in the black and green family tartan, but she liked the soft grey linen suit almost as much, just as she loved this flowing, simple lace dress she was wearing as much as the corseted, fuller wedding gown she had worn in Scotland. No veil this time, just fresh flowers in her hair, her feet bare as she walked through the sand towards the sea, towards her groom, towards her future.

She couldn't believe that it was all real. That this was her life now. The sand squished beneath her bare toes, the sea rippled just a few metres away and the sun beat steadily down, but it all felt like a dream. A perfect dream. It wasn't the future she'd thought she'd wanted but it was a million times better.

Maddison had kept her job at DL Media for the first few months of their engagement while

Kit juggled freelance editing with revitalizing the Buchanan estate, but he had asked her advice so often she had ended up taking a formal role in Scotland, overseeing all the marketing of the estate and its various subsidiaries. It meant spending the bulk of the year in Scotland but Kit had promised they would always return to the beachside cottage here in Bayside for the summers, for Thanksgiving and any other time she wanted to see her sister, and Maddison loved the dramatic Scottish coastline. It felt like home.

The music died down as she reached the end of the aisle and she let go of Savannah's hand, offering hers to Kit instead. How could she feel so shy? Almost unable to look him in the eye. They were already married, after all! But here she was, standing here, in front of the community she had hidden from, run from and returned to, promising once again to worship Kit body and soul and listening to his steady voice promise her the same.

The official closed her book and smiled. 'I now pronounce you husband and wife. You may now kiss the bride.'

Kit's eyes darkened with intent and Maddison's pulse began to race. Their friends and family were all on their feet, clapping, but the sound died away as the blood pounded in her ears and the world narrowed until all she could see was Kit. 'My favourite part,' he murmured as he stepped closer. Maddison quivered as his hands lightly caressed her bare shoulders and he leaned in to brush her mouth with his. She closed her eyes and fell into the deepening kiss, pulling him closer, not wanting the moment to end.

She'd never thought that girls like her would get a happily ever after but today, in this moment, she was more than happy for Kit to prove her wrong—and to keep proving her wrong. Forever.

* * * * *

*If you enjoyed this story,
look for Hope's story,
coming soon!*

MILLS & BOON®
Large Print – September 2016

Morelli's Mistress
Anne Mather

A Tycoon to Be Reckoned With
Julia James

Billionaire Without a Past
Carol Marinelli

The Shock Cassano Baby
Andie Brock

The Most Scandalous Ravensdale
Melanie Milburne

The Sheikh's Last Mistress
Rachael Thomas

Claiming the Royal Innocent
Jennifer Hayward

The Billionaire Who Saw Her Beauty
Rebecca Winters

In the Boss's Castle
Jessica Gilmore

One Week with the French Tycoon
Christy McKellen

Rafael's Contract Bride
Nina Milne

0816 Rom LP